P9-DOE-261

MORE PRAISE

"Paul Levine is guilty of master storytelling in the first degree." —Carl Hiaasen

"Irreverent . . . genuinely clever . . . great fun."
—*New York Times Book Review*

"Mystery writing at its very, very best."
—Larry King, *USA Today*

Trial & Error

A
SOLOMON

vs.
Lord
Novel

Paul Levine

BANTAM BOOKS

TRIAL & ERROR
A Bantam Book / June 2007

Published by
Bantam Dell
A Division of Random House, Inc.
New York, New York

This is a work of fiction. Names, characters, places, and incidents
either are the product of the author's imagination or are used
fictitiously. Any resemblance to actual persons, living or dead,
events, or locales is entirely coincidental.

Bantam Books and the rooster colophon are registered
trademarks of Random House, Inc.

ISBN 978-0-440-24276-5

Printed in the United States of America
Published simultaneously in Canada

www.bantamdell.com

OPM   10 9 8 7 6 5 4 3 2 1

To my grandchildren, Alexandra and Jonah

the fastest Jewish kid on Pine Tree Drive, admittedly a group with more shleppers than sprinters.

He figured there was one chance to catch the man. The channel ran straight for three hundred yards, then dog-legged right for another two hundred yards before reaching open water. He could cut diagonally across an empty field, the shortest leg of the triangle, and intercept the Jet Ski at the inlet to the Bay.

Steve looked back over his shoulder. Bobby had stopped along the seawall, either because he was pooped or because he was belatedly following his uncle's orders.

Steve ran tall, back straight, shoulders relaxed, head still. He had always been fast over short distances. Stealing bases at U of M, a painless ninety-foot sprint. But lousy at distance running. No patience for the training, no tolerance for the pain. Before Victoria, his live-in girlfriend, he'd been a sprinter in his personal life, too. Hundred-yard dashes, hundred-hour relationships.

Flying now, feet barely touching the ground. Hopped over a fallen pond frond, never breaking stride. Shot a look at the Jet Skier, the dive knife sheathed at his ankle. Calculated time and distance. And possible injuries.

Knife wound, concussion, drowning.

They would reach the intersection of channel and Bay simultaneously.

Steve hit the embankment and drove off his back foot. He launched into space, arms spread like wings, soaring toward the man on the Jet Ski, thinking . . .

Just what the hell am I doing?

One

RUNNING TALL

Just after two A.M., Steve Solomon sprinted along the seawall, chasing the man on the Jet Ski.

Black wet suit. Black helmet. Dark visor. A Darth Vader look.

The man shot Steve the bird, then shoved the throttle wide open. The Jet Ski jolted airborne, splashed down, and roared along the channel toward Biscayne Bay.

"Stop him, Uncle Steve!"

Bobby, urging him on. Steve had ordered his twelve-year-old nephew to stay on the dock, but the boy was running, too, trailing behind.

"You can catch him!"

Sure, kiddo. Leave it to me to capture the bad guy, rescue the dolphins, save the world.

A quarter-moon hung like a scythe over the Bay. Cetacean Park should have been quiet. The channel should have rippled placidly in the moist breeze, the air scented with salt and seaweed. Instead, the Jet Ski growled like an angry beast, belching greasy vapors in its wake.

Steve picked up his pace. Years earlier, he had been

Two

FROM BEDROOM TO BAY

One hour before leaping into the darkness of Biscayne Bay, Steve was locked in the spooning position with his girlfriend and law partner, Victoria Lord, her hair tickling his nose, her sweet scent fueling his dreams. The phone jarred him awake. Wade Grisby at Cetacean Park.

Victoria stirred as Steve pulled on his Hurricanes running shorts and a T-shirt with the slogan: *"What If the Hokey Pokey* Is *What It's All About?"*

"Bobby," Steve whispered. Explanation enough.

She rolled over, her blond hair splayed across the pillow. "Dolphins or stars?"

Steve understood the shorthand. Bobby had broken into the planetarium the night of a meteor shower. Lately, the kid had been sneaking out of the house to play with the dolphins on Key Biscayne.

He stroked Victoria's cheek. "Dolphins. Wade Grisby caught him talking to Spunky and Misty."

Talking *and* listening. Bobby believed he could understand dolphinese, as he called it. The boy was even writing a dictionary of the clicks, whistles, and moans that came from their blowholes.

Victoria propped up on one elbow. In her sheer black negligee, with her sleepy eyes, she looked like a star in one of the old black-and-white movies. Lauren Bacall, about to entice her man back to bed.

"Steve, I just can't get enough of you."

Instead, Victoria said, "Steve, maybe it's time Bobby saw a therapist."

"I'll talk to him. He'll be okay."

Steve leaned over and kissed her, Victoria exhaling a warm breath. Asleep before he was out the door.

* * *

Every day another drama, Steve thought, driving across the Rickenbacker Causeway. Getting Bobby out of another jam. This didn't sound as serious as climbing on a catwalk over I-95 to spray paint an exit sign. Bobby had removed the apostrophe from the word "Beaches' " because the typographical error drove him nuts. The kid was sweet and loveable, and in some mysterious way, a genius. But he wasn't socially developed, and lately he'd been acting out.

Breaking curfew. Trespassing. Keeping secrets.

Steve had asked Bobby if everything was okay, if he was having problems, if he wanted to talk about anything.

"Yep."

"Nope."

"Huh?"

Typical adolescent. But unusual for a kid who was ordinarily so verbal. Steve wondered if Bobby's central nervous system disorders were in play. A little klutzy, a lot brainy. The kid seesawed between semi-autistic behavior and savantlike abilities of memory and language feats. "Paradoxical functional facilitation," the doctors called it. Bobby could create anagrams in his head. But lately, his wordplay had been limited to chirping sounds at the breakfast table. Dolphinese.

Steve pulled his Mustang convertible into the empty lot at the bayside attraction. Signs pointed toward the bottlenose dolphin channel, the killer whale tank, the indoor aquarium.

Steve hustled toward the channel. Wondering if he'd been too lax with Bobby, too reluctant to discipline him. Grounding his nephew didn't seem to work. The kid just crawled out his bedroom window and took off.

Steve followed a path of palm trees to the channel. Spotlights on metal poles illuminated the dark water. He figured Grisby would be in his small dockside office, lecturing Bobby on the dangers of breaking into other people's businesses.

That's when Steve heard the roar of the engine. Spotted Darth Vader. Totally surreal.

The Jet Ski carved a turn, kicked up spray, and slowed near the dock. The rider glared at Steve. Early twenties with a pugnacious jaw and cruel mouth. Raising a fist above his head, he shouted, "Liberation!"

What the hell's going on? Where's Grisby? Where's Bobby?

"Bobby!"

Steve heard sneakered footsteps on the concrete dock, his nephew running toward him, all flying elbows and knees, a skinny arm pointing at the masked man on the Jet Ski. "He's stealing Spunky and Misty!"

The man cruised close to the seawall and bared his teeth. "Freedom for the animals!"

So that's it. The guy's a dolphin-kidnapping, animal-libbing, eco-terrorist asshole.

Steve was all for animal rights. But not burning

down labs. Or bombing research centers. Or terrorizing scientists. If a few rats had to die to find a cure for cancer—well, it was a trade-off that made sense.

The man gave Steve the finger, gunned the Jet Ski, and headed out the channel toward the Bay.

"Stop him, Uncle Steve!"

Three

CALL ME FISHMEAL

One hour before Bobby Solomon begged his uncle to stop Darth Vader from stealing the two dolphins, the boy had climbed a chain-link fence, sneaked across a concrete dock, and crept over a catwalk to a floating wooden platform.

Praying he wouldn't be caught.

Uncle Steve would be so pissed. But Bobby had decided to take the risk.

I need to talk to Misty and Spunky.

His best friends.

Waiting for their signal, Bobby sprawled on his back. He let his eyes grow accustomed to the dark. In a moment, he spotted the constellation Sagittarius in the clear night sky.

A splash, then a rapid-fire *click-creak-click*. A second splash and a familiar high-pitched whistle.

Misty and Spunky saying hello.

They were the stars at Cetacean Park. Spunky was the color of a blue-steel revolver, with a long beak and a gray belly. His fluke—the wing-shaped paddle at the end of his tail—was oversize, powering his giant leaps.

He weighed about 250 pounds, depending on how much mackerel he'd had for breakfast. Misty, his girl-friend, had a sleek, silvery-blue body with a pink belly. She loved to be rubbed at the base of her dorsal fin.

Bobby put two fingers to his lips and whistled. Two short blasts. *"Hi guys."*

Spunky slapped the water with a fin, splashing Bobby. The Spunkster joking around.

No tanks to confine them, the two dolphins lived in a channel that ran to Biscayne Bay, a steel gate block-ing their path to open water. Bobby swam with the dolphins, fed them, played with them. Even watched them have sex, belly-to-belly.

Not an everyday sighting. Not like seeing Pamela Anderson or Paris Hilton do the big nasty on video.

Pennants strung across the channel crackled in the sea breeze. The park had been closed for hours, but sugary songs about a thousand years old still poured from the speakers. Barbra Streisand was ordering someone not to rain on her parade. Barbra Streisand. SAD BREAST BRAIN.

So easy. You just picture the letters, and they fly around and anagrammatize themselves. Bobby thought in pictures and sounds, just like the dolphins. He could remember almost everything he'd ever seen or heard.

For the past year, he'd been listening to the sounds coming from Spunky's and Misty's blowholes, trying to untangle their language. Building a dictionary of dolphin talk. The clicks and squeaks, moans and whis-tles all meant something, but you had to be patient. You had to *really* listen and remember the patterns. Tonight, he hoped to add a few new phrases to his notebook. Then he'd bicycle home, sneak back into the house without waking Uncle Steve and Victoria, and catch some z's before school.

Earlier tonight, he'd told Victoria a big fat fib. More than one, really. She'd been cooking meat loaf, filled with onions and dripping with Worcestershire and Tabasco sauce. She wouldn't eat a bite, but she always made meals Bobby loved. That's the way Victoria was. Making sure his clothes were clean, his homework finished, his hair combed. So he was bummed to fake her out.

She'd been worried about him, Bobby knew. Tonight, he promised not to break curfew, not to sneak out, not to slink into places he didn't belong. Then, when she came into his bedroom around eleven P.M., while Uncle Steve was watching *Sports Center*, Bobby pretended to be asleep. Victoria sat on the edge of his bed, stroked his hair, and sang a lullaby to him. "Goodnight, My Angel," the Billy Joel song. Like he was a little kid, except no one ever sang to him when he was little, including his real mom, who—let's face it—was basically a coke whore who didn't care about anyone but herself.

As Victoria sang, Bobby squeezed his eyes shut and bit his lower lip to keep from crying. Wishing she was his mom. Hoping Uncle Steve didn't blow it with her.

Now, two hours after Victoria pulled the blanket up to his chin and softly closed his bedroom door, Bobby lay on the floating platform at Cetacean Park. After a few moments, Misty swam up to him.

Bobby *click-clack*ed his tongue. *"Hungry, Misty?"*

She whistled a two-syllable reply. *"Feed me."*

That's what it sounded like, anyway. Bobby reached into a rubber pail and lobbed a chunk of mackerel toward the water. Misty gulped it down and whistled again. *"Thanks."*

He dug into the pail for another fish, and chirped a high-pitched sound from the back of his throat. *"Squid or crab, Spunky?"*

"Who's there?"

Oh, shit. Mr. Grisby.

Bobby could see the owner of Cetacean Park, silhouetted by a spotlight on the dock. A nice guy—but then, he'd never caught Bobby breaking into the place.

"Goddammit! Answer me! I know you're there."

And if Uncle Steve finds out . . .

Bobby peered through the darkness, his heart pounding. Mr. Grisby was holding something in both hands. A rifle? A shotgun? No, why would he . . . ?

"Who the hell's there!"

Southern accent. Sounding riled.

Bobby pressed down flat on the platform. It was hard to tell in the spotlight's glare, but Mr. Grisby seemed to be looking his way.

"Dammit! Answer me."

Nowhere to swim, nowhere to hide.

A thunderclap. Spunky broke the surface, twirled a backflip ten feet above the waterline, hung in the air a second, then hit the surface with a quiet *splash.* Showing off, but blowing Bobby's cover, too.

On the speakers, Celine Dion was singing, "My Heart Will Go On." Somewhere, Bobby thought, a big ship was about to sideswipe an iceberg. Celine Dion. END ICON LIE.

Spunky surfaced and whistled. A trilling *wee-o, wee-o, wee-o.* Calling Misty, Bobby knew. Then another sound. Not the dolphin.

A sliding metallic *clack.*

Bobby knew that sound. He'd gone skeet shooting with his grandpop.

A shotgun racking.

"Last chance, dammit! You, on the platform! Hands up!"

"Don't shoot, Mr. Grisby." Bobby's voice wobbled.

"Robert Solomon. That you?"

"Yes, sir." Bobby got to one knee, raised his hands in surrender.

Grisby chuckled. "Dammit, boy. Your uncle know where you are?"

"No, sir. I sneaked out."

"Gonna call him right now. I'll bet he tans your hide before the sun comes up."

"Uncle Steve doesn't believe in spanking."

"Then he's a damn fool."

A blast of water. Spunky and Misty exploded above the surface, side by side. The dolphins' bodies were silvery-black against the moonlight. They hit the surface together, smooth as knives, and vanished.

They had heard something, Bobby thought. Or sensed it with their sonar. What we call "sonar," anyway. Their echolocation ability. Sending out sound waves, getting readings back. Seeing in the dark by picturing the shapes of objects.

So totally cool to be a dolphin. To swim so fast, dive so deep, jump so high.

Bobby wondered what they sensed in the darkness. Mr. Grisby stared out at the channel, toward the open water of the Bay. Bobby followed his gaze. Nothing there.

"I want you out of here quick." Grisby didn't take his eyes from the horizon.

Bobby heard something in the man's voice. Saw it as

a picture, felt it on his skin. Something cold and sharp, an icicle poking him in the back.

"Dammit, boy! You hear me? This is no place for you."

The sound a freezing liquid now, covering Bobby as if he were encased in a glacier. It was the sound of fear.

Four

GUNSHOTS IN THE DARK

A flood of sensations as Steve flew off the embankment toward Darth Vader on the Jet Ski. The metal gate at the Bay inlet, marked with red and green lights, was wide open. If the bastard made it through the inlet, he'd have a clear path all the way to Key West. Then, in the distance, another Jet Ski, already in the Bay. An accomplice. And silhouetted in the headlight of the Jet Ski, two dolphins sped into open water.

Shit. Too late to rescue them.

Steve was airborne.

Spread-eagled.

The masked man ducked. The crook of Steve's right arm caught him under the chin, cartwheeled him off the Jet Ski. A clothesline tackle.

A second later, both men were treading water, the Jet Ski purring softly, turning tight circles in the channel. Steve's right shoulder flared with pain. It felt as if someone had stabbed him with an ice pick, then hammered it into the bone. Next to him, the man's hand was clapped protectively over his neck.

A thick neck. Strong jaw with high cheekbones. Light-skinned African-American. His helmet had been knocked off, revealing a shaved head. Illuminated only by the moon and the lights on the gate, the guy looked a little like that wrestler turned actor. The Rock. Dwayne Johnson, the guy who gave all that money to the University of Miami.

"Corporate goon," the man groaned.

Steve treaded water and massaged his right shoulder. "Hey, asshole. You scared the shit out of my nephew."

"You don't think dolphins are scared when they're taken from their mothers?"

"Don't start that crap with me."

The two men faced each other in the water, each pedaling to stay afloat. On the causeway, a police siren wailed.

"You think your nephew's life has more value than a dolphin's? Or a turtle's? Or a harbor rat's?"

"As a matter of fact, I do." No use telling this guy, but Steve valued Bobby's life more than his own.

"You're with them, aren't you?" the man demanded.

"Them who?"

"The circuses and the zoos. The testers and the torturers. The users and abusers."

"I'm just a guy with a nephew who loves dolphins."

The man reached under the water and came up with the dive knife that had been sheathed at his ankle. Serrated blade, glimmery in the moonlight. With his free hand, he started paddling toward the Jet Ski. "Try to stop me, I'll cut your throat."

"Isn't my life worth as much as a harbor rat's?"

A light blazed, blinding Steve. "Hold it right there! Both of you!" boomed overhead.

Steve squinted toward the shore. Police car on the bank. Two cops at the water's edge. One gripped a

Maglite the size of a Barry Bonds bat. The other aimed his 9 mm Glock at them. Two-handed grip, legs spread and knees flexed, just like they teach them at the academy.

Steve continued treading water.

"Hands where I can see 'em!"

What's the cop think I'm gonna do, the backstroke?

Steve threw both hands above his head. He immediately sank. He kicked hard and popped up just as Darth Vader called the cops "establishment thugs."

"For the record," Steve interjected, spitting water, "I play softball in the Police Athletic League."

One cop started to say something but was interrupted by the blast of a shotgun, the sound rolling down the channel. Instinctively, Steve whirled toward the park.

Bobby! Where's Bobby?

The last Steve had seen the boy, he had stopped along the seawall, waiting for his uncle to be a hero.

An instant later, a second blast echoed in the warm ocean breeze.

SOLOMON'S LAWS

1. Try not to piss off a cop unless you have a damn good reason . . . or a damn good lawyer.

Five

ANOTHER PERP

The cops cuffed Steve and slammed him facedown onto the hood of the cruiser. Water dripped down his legs into his Reeboks.

All that mattered was Bobby, and Steve couldn't get to him. "C'mon, man. My nephew's back there."

"How many of you are there?" the bigger cop demanded.

"I'm not one of them!" Steve lifted his head. A hand slammed it back down. Steve's eyes teared and his nose dripped blood. A fire burned deep in his shoulder. "Did you hear the gunshots? I gotta find Bobby."

"Shut up." The cop clipped the back of Steve's skull with his Maglite. Just a practice swing. Steve decided he didn't want to feel the real thing.

"Don't they teach you in cop school that gunshots are bad?" Steve asked.

"Got other units there." The cop was going through the soggy contents of Steve's wallet. Seventeen dollars, a year-old Fantasy 5 lottery ticket, and his Florida Bar card. "You're a lawyer."

"Yeah, and you're gonna need one."

Steve liked most cops, even the ones who stretched the truth in their testimony, forcing him to cross-examine the crap out of them. They had their job to do, and he had his, which was to make them look like idiots or liars. Or both.

These two were young. One Hispanic, one black. Both with sleeves tight against bulging biceps.

Don't they test cops for steroids the way they do ballplayers?

It was something he'd look into the next time some cop roughed up one of his presumably innocent clients. *'Roid rage.*

"My nephew's got a medical condition. So if you could be a pal and—"

"Shut up," the Hispanic cop repeated. His partner separately questioned Darth Vader over by a scrubby palm tree. Steve couldn't hear the questions, but several answers seemed to include the words "Gestapo thug" and "global corporate conspiracy," sprinkled with mentions of Abu Ghraib and Guantanamo.

Steve explained how Grisby called him about Bobby, how he drove to Cetacean Park, stumbled into an animal liberation raid, chased this yahoo in the wet suit, then saw a second Jet Skier, who'd already made it to the Bay with two dolphins.

"Another perp," the cop said, sounding interested. "You get a look at him?"

Steve shook his head, water dripping from his hair. "Too dark. Too far away. He was herding the dolphins into open water, and that jerkoff was bringing up the rear."

The radio in the squad car crackled, and the Hispanic cop ducked inside to take the call. When he emerged, he said, "Is it safe to assume your nephew's not around forty years old, maybe two hundred pounds?"

"He's twelve and built like a broomstick."

"Good. Then he's not the dead guy."

HABEAS PORPOISE

They drove back to Cetacean Park in the cruiser, along an unpaved access road. The cops told Steve everything they knew from the radio call. Wade Grisby had shot someone, another guy in a wet suit. A third perp, the cop said. It happened on a path near the security shed. Steve's nephew wasn't near the shooting, didn't even see it happen. The kid was talking to a detective now. He was just fine.

Steve felt the relief immediately. If Victoria was his heart, Bobby was his soul. Eighteen months earlier, Steve had risked everything to rescue the boy—kidnap him, really—from his own mother. Janice Solomon, Steve's drug-addled sister, was an abusive parent and a pathological liar, and those were her best qualities. When Bobby came to live with Steve, the boy was terrified and helpless, plagued by night terrors, his psyche a scrambled mess. Steve decided then that he'd do anything to make the kid's life better. Bobby had made great progress, but not without some setbacks. Overall, the kid was so sweet and innocent he gave Steve faith in the goodness of the species, notwithstanding all evidence to the contrary.

Three more police cars and an ambulance angled alongside the seawall, lights flashing. A covey of cops in uniform and two others in plainclothes milled about. A fire-rescue vehicle was pulling up, two EMTs leaping out. On the causeway, another siren wailed.

A few yards from the killer whale tank, Bobby sat in the front row of the bleachers, wrapped in a pink beach towel, sipping soda from a can. A Miami-Dade sheriff's deputy Steve recognized from the Justice Building took notes on a pad. "Then Uncle Steve took off after the guy," Bobby said, his voice stoked. "You shoulda seen him. Awesome! Like a zillion miles an hour."

"Hey, kiddo. You okay?" Steve scooped up his nephew and hugged him.

"Did you catch him? 'Cause they should pay you a big reward, a big chunk of cheddar."

The deputy held up a hand. "Give us a minute, Mr. Solomon."

Steve studied his nephew. "Sure you're okay, Bobby?"

"Abso-posi-tutely. But where are Spunky and Misty?"

"In the Bay somewhere."

Bobby's expression froze. The energy drained from him.

"Where in the Bay?"

"I don't know, kiddo. They were headed for the southern tip of the Key."

Meaning they could be in the deep, blue Atlantic by now, but Steve chose not to say that.

"Can you find them, Uncle Steve?" Fear in his voice. "Can you get them back?"

"I'll try, kiddo."

How, I don't know. A writ of habeas porpoise, maybe.

"Please, Uncle Steve."

"Gonna do my best."

"Not enough!"

"What?"

"Not enough. Not enough. Not enough. I want them back. Now!"

Whining. Swaying. His mouth contorted. The old Bobby. Insecure and frightened. Bobby had made so much progress, had become so socialized, it was difficult to remember the skin-and-bones, bruised and grimy kid locked in a dog cage, his legs festering with open sores.

Steve picked up Bobby. The boy slung his legs around his uncle and locked his ankles together. Steve gave him a squeeze and whispered in his ear, "It's gonna be okay, kiddo."

"Sure." He didn't sound convinced.

Steve felt teardrops roll from Bobby's cheek to his own. "I know how much Spunky and Misty mean to you. They're like the brother and sister you don't have."

"You could change that," Bobby said.

"How?"

"You and Victoria, I mean."

"Oh, that. Let's get the dolphins back first, then we'll discuss whether the world needs any more Solomons."

"Deal," Bobby said. Sounding better. He untangled himself from Steve, rubbed his nose with a thumb, and turned back to the deputy. "Would you like to hear the rest of my statement now, Officer?"

Sounding like an expert witness who'd been doing this for years. That was Bobby for you. One moment a babbling kid, a second later he'd name every turnpike stop from Homestead to St. Lucie.

"You sure you're okay?" Steve asked.

"Go," Bobby said. "Maybe you can pick up some clues."

Steve left Bobby with the deputy and headed toward a semicircle of cops on the path that led to the security shed. Two large feet in rubber dive booties stuck out of a low hedge of ficus trees.

Moving closer, Steve caught sight of the body. A man in a black wet suit, just like the one worn by the Jet Skier. The man lay on his back in a pool of blood. A deep pool. More blood than it seemed any one body could hold. The man's chest had been blown wide open. Shotgun blast at close range. Ugly.

A second blast—or more likely the first—had torn through the man's right hip. Near his feet was a roll of duct tape, flecked with gore and body tissue. A small coil of nautical line curled near one knee. A police photographer hovered over the corpse, snapping off rapid-fire pictures.

Two plainclothes detectives stood nearby, listening to Wade Grisby, who sucked at a cigarette, his leathery hands trembling. "A man's got a right to defend himself, don't he?"

Grisby was in his early fifties, short and wiry, with sunbaked skin and a gray-flaked beard. He looked up as Steve approached. "This fellow knows me. Tell them, Steve. I wouldn't shoot a man unless it was self-defense."

Steve joined the circle. "Wade, you might not want to make any more statements until you have a lawyer."

"I got nothing to hide."

"Still, Wade. It's time to lawyer up."

Steve was about to announce his own availability at reasonable rates when he heard a familiar voice. "Don't need a mouthpiece when you got the po-lice."

Mellifluous tones. Bourbon flowing over ice.

Steve turned and saw Ray Pincher striding toward them. The State Attorney wore a dark suit and a dress shirt, leaving off only the tie, perhaps a concession to the pre-dawn hour. Pincher was a fit African-American man in his forties with a narrow mustache and an irritating habit of cracking his knuckles to emphasize that he'd just made an important point. He'd grown up in the Liberty City projects and won some amateur boxing titles as a middleweight before heading off to a seminary in Jacksonville. The idea was to return home as pastor of the Primitive Baptist Church. But somewhere along the line, Ray Pincher lost his faith and found the law. A tough prosecutor who'd paid his dues from Traffic Court to the Homicide Division, he now was the county's elected State Attorney.

"Ain't no suspense when it's self-defense." Pincher sounded part rap artist, part preacher. He signaled Steve to walk with him. "If you're hustling a case, Solomon, forget about it. Grisby was within his rights. He'll never be charged."

"That's it? You're here all of one minute and you know what happened?"

"We been keeping an eye on this place."

"You had men here tonight?"

"A mile away. Sewage plant on Virginia Key."

Right. Virginia Key. A place of natural dunes and beautiful beaches. Turtles and manatees. Hardwood hammocks and mangroves. Naturally, it's where the city *padres* built a sewage treatment plant. Even though it was hidden from sight, when the wind was right, you could smell it from the causeway.

"Animal Liberation Movement," Pincher said. "Bunch of losers and lefties. Once they knocked over that primate lab in the Keys, we figured Grisby's place might be next." Pincher cracked his knuckles with a *crunch*.

"Who's the dead guy?"

"Don't have an ID yet."

"Why'd he come ashore?"

"Looks like he planned to tie up the security guard. Instead, he ran into Grisby and his twelve-guage."

"Was the guy armed?"

"A .45. Gun flew into the ficus hedge when he was hit."

"The timing's off. The dolphins were already gone when the shots were fired."

"Grisby was holding the guy, waiting for us to get here. The guy went for his piece."

"Who does that? If someone's holding a twelve-gauge on you, would you pull a gun?"

"Didn't say the guy was smart. Only said he was dead."

"And why two shots? Guy would have bled out with either one."

"What's with you, Solomon? You want Grisby indicted so you can get some work?"

"I'm just wondering why you're closing the book on this. You've got no independent witnesses. But you've wrapped up your investigation while the body's still warm."

"And what's it to you?"

Good question. Steve wasn't sure why the story troubled him. He was a defense lawyer to his very core, so his natural instincts were to believe Grisby acted in self-defense. But Pincher was a prosecutor to the depth of *his* soul, and he never believed anyone. Why so quick to clear the man in a brutal shooting?

But what the hell. None of this concerned him.

All I care is that Bobby's safe.

"Means nothing to me, Ray. Nothing at all."

Pincher led Steve toward the patrol car where the two muscle-bound cops still had the first perp in the backseat. "The asshole say anything I might want to know?" Pincher asked Steve.

"Like I told Tubbs and Crockett here, all he did was call me names."

The Hispanic cop nodded to Pincher, then opened the back door of the cruiser. The man leaned out, his chiseled features illuminated by the ceiling lamp.

Pincher stood, paralyzed. "What the fuck?"

Looking delighted with himself, the man grinned at Pincher. "Hello, Uncle Ray. Mom says hi, too."

Pincher clenched his jaws so tightly, Steve heard his teeth grind. "Solomon, say hello to Gerald Nash, my sister's punk-ass boy."

"We've already met," Steve said.

Pincher wagged a finger in Nash's face. "Your momma shoulda whupped your ass, 'stead of taking all that sass."

"You're just a tool of the establishment, Uncle Ray. A tiny cog in the wheel of corrupt corporations and warmongering politicians."

"I hear your daddy talking. All that left-wing bull-shit."

"Dad's always been right about you, Uncle Ray. You're just a puppet."

"You were mine, Gerald, I woulda taught you some discipline."

"I learned a lot from you, Uncle Ray." Hands cuffed behind him, Gerald Nash scooted around in his seat, laced his fingers together, and cracked his knuckles. Then he cackled with laughter.

"How funny's it gonna be when you're doing life in Raiford?" his uncle demanded.

"Life, Uncle Ray? For trespassing? Breaking and entering? I don't think so."

Pincher turned his back on Nash. "Solomon, tell this punk the news."

Steve didn't relish being ordered around by his old antagonist. Still, it had been a long night and he didn't mind rubbing Nash's face in the mud. "It's called 'felony murder.' Wade Grisby might have shot your pal, but you're the one who'll go down for it."

Seven

ALL STEVE, ALL THE TIME

"Let me get this straight," Judge Frederick Barash said. "You're suing this website where men comment on women they've dated."

"Don't Date the Bitch–dot-com," Victoria Lord said, trying not to reveal her embarrassment. She hated cleaning up Steve's messes, handling cases for his low-rent clients. "The website posted insulting and derogatory remarks about our client, Your Honor."

The judge licked his thumb and riffled through the complaint. "To wit, that Ms. Lexy Larson is 'a shallow, superficial gold digger who gives perfunctory blow jobs.'"

Judge Barash *harrumph*ed and peered over the tops of his reading glasses toward the plaintiff's table. He had served twenty-seven years on the bench and was a few months shy of retirement. A small man with a fine crop of judicial white hair, His Honor would have dismissed every case on his docket if he could, just to play golf every day. You could almost smell the burnout.

"That's what our complaint alleges," Victoria said, referring to Steve's sloppily worded written pleading. Sitting alongside was her client—actually, Steve's client—Lexy Larson, a six-foot-tall model with spiky blond hair.

" 'Perfunctory,' " the judge mused. "Not a word usually associated with blow jobs, is it?"

"Is that a grammatical question or a personal one, Your Honor?" Victoria shot back.

Dammit, Steve. From now on, handle your own crap.

"Don't get your undies in an uproar, Ms. Lord. Just tell me, what's libelous here? 'Superficial gold digger' or 'perfunctory blow job'?"

This is not happening to me.

"Perfunctory?" Lexy whispered, her face scrunched up. "Is that like sloppy? Because I can give head wet or dry." She made a *slurp*ing sound.

This is so not happening to me.

Back at Yale, Victoria had envisioned herself a top trial lawyer, winning major cases, dispensing her opinions on Court TV. In her organized, methodical way, she had charted a path. Five years as a prosecutor, trying hundreds of cases, building a name. Another ten years in a private firm, making some serious money. Finally, the bench. Public service.

"Judge Lord." It had a ring to it.

Never did she imagine she'd be debating the quality of fellatio performed by a model with a two-digit IQ.

"Sometimes, I spit on the guy's cock," Lexy whispered, fidgeting in her chair. "But some guys, if it's too slippery, they claim they don't feel a thing."

"Shhh." Victoria placed a hand on Lexy's bare, artificially tanned and superbly toned arm. The model wore a leopard-print strapless cotton sundress, and her oiled skin was goose-bumpy in the meat-locker-cold courtroom. A jumbo Fendi crocodile purse sat next to her feet, which were shod in red patent leather Mizrahi mules. A great outfit for a drink at the Delano, but Victoria would have preferred something more conservative for court. Still, as Lexy usually dressed like a Victoria's Secret model—which, in fact, she was—it could have been worse.

Lexy was one of the *moe-dels*—her pronunciation—from Les Mannequins, the second-rate agency where Solomon & Lord enjoyed free office space in return for legal counsel. When Steve had rolled in just before dawn, bruised and still wet, he'd asked Victoria to handle his morning calendar. Meaning she had to oppose the motion to dismiss the libel suit, a case as flimsy as the gold mesh bra peeking out of Lexy's dress.

"Let's take a look at what else is posted on the website," the judge said, turning a page, then reading aloud, " 'Don't date a bitch named Lexy, a SoBe model with mud for brains. She's a vapid, vacuous airhead who drinks Cristal by the magnum, which she'll charge to your platinum card.' "

"Creepskate," Lexy murmured.

Meaning, Victoria figured, a guy who was both cheap *and* a creep.

"Now, Ms. Lord," the judge continued, "*did* your client charge champagne to this man's credit card?"

"Yes, Your Honor," Victoria admitted.

Not to mention ordering two rounds of drinks for a table of strangers, a twenty-four-ounce porterhouse steak for herself, of which she ate two bites, and a four-pound lobster "to go" for her Himalayan kitty, Veruschka.

"Then I don't see how you can maintain an action for libel," Judge Barash said. "All the other comments are statements of opinion, and the law says there's no such thing as a false opinion."

"Nine out of ten guys say I give great head," Lexy hissed in Victoria's ear.

"Hush," Victoria cautioned, using one of her mother's favorite words. She turned toward the bench. "Your Honor, by posting intimate, personal information, the website invaded Ms. Larson's privacy."

"I don't believe your complaint makes that allegation," the judge replied.

Your complaint being Steve's flabbily worded pleading. He'd probably dictated it without a minute of legal research. Or maybe he'd just let Cece Santiago, their assistant/secretary/personal trainer, write the damn thing. Either way, it was a mess, just like Steve's underwear drawer.

"In that case, Your Honor, I would consent to a dismissal without prejudice in order to file an amended complaint stating a cause of action for invasion of privacy."

"Excellent idea, Ms. Lord." Doubtless thinking he'd be retired to Hilton Head before this lame lawsuit came to trial.

"What's happening?" Lexy demanded. "Whadaya mean, 'dismissal'?"

"Everything's fine. Go to your Pilates class. I'll rewrite the complaint for Steve."

"Where is that cutie? He should have been here."

Lexy said it with a little whimper that men probably found enchanting.

"Like I told you, Lexy, the cutie had a hard night."

When he had dropped into bed, Steve mumbled something about trouble at Cetacean Park.

"What kind of trouble?"

"Later. Sleep now."

He started snoring then, a sound vaguely reminiscent, Victoria decided, of the whistles made by Bobby's dolphins. When she dressed for court, Steve was still snoring. She checked on Bobby, curled up in his own bed, breathing heavily. As she left the house, she saw Bobby's bicycle sticking out of the trunk of Steve's car.

This was the third time in a month the boy had sneaked out, and Victoria was worried. He'd been making progress, seeming to adjust so well. But then his fascination with dolphins pushed everything else aside. He was obsessed with the animals, and it didn't seem healthy.

"Ms. Lord," the judge said, "I wonder if you could join me in chambers a moment."

Now what?

"Is there a problem, Your Honor?"

"Not with this pipsqueak of a case." The judge eased out of his chair and headed for the door behind the bench, tossing over his shoulder, "A murder trial, Counselor."

What murder trial?

The firm of Solomon & Lord didn't have any. These days, their clients were mostly Whiplash Willies and hapless misdemeanants. Steve's job was to hustle most of the cases. But as a rainmaker, he was more of a drizzler.

They'd also had a run of bad luck. Just last week, a jury rejected their client's claim that he was sleepwalking when he entered the liquor store with gun in hand. When the judge sentenced him to seven years in prison, the jerk said he'd rather get eight years, because 8 was Daunte Culpepper's jersey number, and the quarterback was his favorite Miami Dolphin, even if he was over the hill. Victoria started to protest, but Steve said he was just thankful the guy's favorite player wasn't Jason Taylor. It took Victoria a second to realize that Steve meant Taylor wore number 99.

Something else had been bothering her lately, too.

Can there be too much togetherness?

Working together and living together. Sharing an office and sharing a bed. All Steve, all the time. She loved Steve—but she didn't love working with him.

She feared that their professional life was beginning to threaten their personal life, but what to do about it? She'd even toyed with the idea of opening her own shop, but when she'd raised the idea, Steve had sulked for days.

"We're a team," Steve told her. "Just like the cobra and the mongoose."

"The cobra and the mongoose fight each other to the death," she said.

"See. That's why we're so great together. I paint the big picture. You point out the details."

Eight

THE RIGHT WOMAN
FOR THE JOB

Judge Barash was hanging up his robe when Victoria walked in. The chambers had the requisite oak desk, heavy crimson drapes, floor-to-ceiling bookshelves, and handsome Persian rug. Standing at the bookshelves, a man fiddled with a brass model of the scales of justice, tilting them out of whack like a butcher with a heavy thumb.

Ray Pincher. What's he doing here?

"Ms. Lord," the judge said, "I'm sure you know the State Attorney."

"I worked for Mr. Pincher," she replied, omitting the fact that he'd fired her.

"Ms. Lord was still green then," Pincher said. Victoria wondered if that was an apology.

The State Attorney wore a jet-black suit with a silk burgundy shirt and matching tie. Pincher's cuff links—miniature handcuffs—rattled as he played with the scales. He had a military officer's posture and projected both self-confidence and self-righteousness.

"I assume Solomon told you what happened out on the Key in the wee hours," Pincher said to Victoria.

Omigod. What had Steve said? Trouble at Cetacean Park. What now?

"Is Steve in any trouble?" she asked.

"For once, no. Actually, inconceivably, he's sort of a semi-hero."

Pincher took several minutes explaining that the Animal Liberation Movement, the ALM, had been terrorizing zoos and tourist attractions and research labs for months. Last night, they'd hit Cetacean Park. Three guys. One got away. Steve helped nab one of the others, though Pincher made it sound more like an accident.

"Wade Grisby, the owner of the place, shot the third terrorist," Pincher said. "Killed him. Clear case of self-defense."

"Meaning the Grand Jury will indict the guy Solomon caught," Judge Barash chimed in. "Thank God I don't have to preside over that can of worms."

"Felony murder," Victoria said.

Pincher nodded. "You got it."

One of the quirks in the law. If you and your buddy rob a convenience store, and the owner kills your buddy, you're guilty of felony murder because your crime—robbery—precipitated the shooting. Makes no difference that the victim is your partner in crime and maybe deserved it.

"What's all this have to do with me?" Victoria asked.

"Bad guy's a dumb ass, and I gotta pass," Pincher said.

Victoria's look posed a question that Pincher quickly answered. "His name's Gerald Nash, and that sucker's my sister's boy."

"You're conflicted out," she said.

"Me and my whole office."

"But what's that got to do with me?" she repeated. Her eyes flicked from Pincher to the judge and back again. "You're not saying you want *me* to prosecute?"

Pincher cracked his knuckles. "You're the right woman for the job."

"I'm ready to administer the oath," Judge Barash announced. "Got the Bible right here."

Double-teaming me. What's going on?

Victoria looked straight at Pincher. "I don't get it. All the lawyers in Miami, you choose me to prosecute your nephew? You don't even like me."

"I don't like *Solomon*. Got no problem with you."

"You *fired* me."

"Had to set an example. You caused a mistrial, embarrassed my office."

Not as much as the whole episode had embarrassed her, Victoria thought. It was her first encounter with Steve-the-Shark Solomon, defense lawyer. She was prosecuting a bird-smuggler, and Steve called a white-feathered cockatoo to testify. Victoria had lost her cool, and Steve gleefully baited her into a mistrial. Not only that, but the bird crapped on the sleeve of her Gucci jacket.

"You've matured since then," Pincher continued. "And I've always felt a little guilty about canning you."

"Uh-huh." Not buying it.

"You'll get lots of press, make a name for yourself, bring in some paying clients." Pincher gave her a sharp smile and cracked his knuckles again. "Let someone else rep the sleepwalkers who rob liquor stores."

"If I lose, people will say you appointed me to cut your nephew a break."

"I despise the little bastard. A self-righteous prick

just like his old man. And you won't lose. Gerald broke into Cetacean Park. His accomplice was killed. Close the book. He's on the hook."

In her brief tenure as a prosecutor, Victoria had never handled a murder trial. But Pincher couldn't be tanking the case. The political fallout would be brutal. And he was right. *State* v. *Nash* was a slam dunk. Pincher was right about something else, too. A high-profile case was just what Solomon & Lord needed. And even better, she could work on her own. Solo, without Steve hovering over her, second-guessing every tactical decision.

So, despite the uneasy feeling of not knowing precisely what was going on, Victoria turned to the judge and said, "Where's that Bible, Your Honor?"

SOLOMON'S LAWS

2. The best way to hustle a case is to pretend you don't want the work.

Nine

STUPIDITY IN THE FIRST
DEGREE

Gerald Nash—aka Darth Vader, aka Pincher's nephew—gave Steve a wiseass grin. "Why do you think I called you?"

"Let's see," Steve said. "You're in jail. I'm a defense lawyer. I don't know. Why?"

"So you're not surprised?"

"I've been trying cases ten years. I'm only surprised when clients tell the truth."

They were sitting in a brightly lit yet grim interview room at the Miami-Dade County jail. The scuffed walls were painted pea-soup green and the furniture—scarred wooden table, straight-backed chairs—was the stuff of one-room schoolhouses. The place smelled of metal, lubricants, and sweat. Heavy doors *clank*ed and buzzers sounded from inside the old hellhole.

"So why do you want to represent me?" Nash challenged Steve.

In the light, Nash bore some resemblance to Pincher. Lighter skinned than his uncle, but the same pugnacious jaw. A similarity in personalities, too. Just like the State Attorney, Nash projected arrogance and self-righteousness.

"Who says I want to represent you?" Steve fired back. "I like Wade Grisby, and you just screwed up his business."

"He treats the dolphins as if he owns them."

"He *does* own them. He caught them or bought them or bred them. Now he feeds them and trains them."

"Sounds like a slave owner in the Old South."

"Disabled kids swim with the dolphins for therapy, and Grisby doesn't charge them a dime. The way I see it, he's helping humanity, and you're a worthless punk."

"His park is nothing more than a chlorinated prison."

"Bullshit. The dolphins get all-you-can-eat sushi. They have medical care. They love the people there."

"You have no idea what dolphins feel."

"And *you* do?"

"Have you ever run your hand over a dolphin's belly, all wet and slippery?"

Nash said it with such a rhapsodic look, he might have been stroking Angelina Jolie's ass.

"They're gorgeous animals, anatomically perfect," Nash continued. "They can swim twenty-five miles an hour and dive to a thousand feet. But you know what's best about them?"

"They're not sharks?"

"They live at peace in a harmonious society."

"I wonder if the fish they eat would agree."

"Did you know bottleneck dolphins have their own language?"

"Yeah, my nephew told me. He thinks he understands them. He also thinks you should be shot. He's gonna be pissed if I represent you."

"Why?"

"The dolphins you released are his pals."

"Then he should be thrilled. Dolphins in captivity grow obese. They fill up with the junk food the stupid tourists throw them. They don't hunt. They don't dive. They need to be free."

"You know what you are, Nash? A true believer. A self-appointed savior. And that makes you really dangerous."

"This the way you get your cases, Solomon? Insult the client?"

"I don't need the work, Nash."

Technically, that was true, Steve thought. He could be working, pro bono, on any number of cases for Lexy and Rexy, the twin bimbo models, who spent as much time litigating as posing. For the umpteenth time, Lexy had been ticketed for parking in a handicap zone, despite Steve's warning that bulimia did not qualify. He was also fending off lawsuits against her sister, Rexy, who had a habit of selling costume jewelry as the real thing on eBay. Rexy claimed innocence on the grounds that the cheap jewelry had been worn by a semi-famous SoBe model, her very own self, and therefore it took on additional value.

"So why are you here?" Nash asked. "Why aren't you in the courthouse with all those clients of yours?"

A perfectly good question. Steve had awakened around eleven, pulled on jeans and a T-shirt with the slogan: *"Speak Slowly. I'm Not Fluent in Idiot."* He took Bobby to school, figuring half a day of sixth-grade education was better than none. Cece, his secretary or assistant or office czarina, or whatever the hell she called herself this week, phoned to say that a jail inmate named Gerald Nash wanted to see him.

Despite his posturing, Steve wanted the case of *State v. Nash*. Not that he liked Nash. But that was okay. Maybe even better. If you're fond of your clients, it's harder on you when they're carted off to prison.

If he got the case, Steve would have to explain some things to Bobby. He'd tell the boy that guilt isn't black or white. The legal system is filled with shades of gray. Gerald Nash was more misguided than dangerous. Should he be put away forever based on the dumbest thing he ever did? Steve believed in the power of people to change. Okay, maybe not serial killers. But if he was spared prison, Gerald Nash *might* change his life. Maybe he'd work in animal rescue and give up the felonious stuff.

Then there's the little matter of the felony murder rule, a hoary remnant of the English Common Law. Sure, Nash was responsible for the loss of Misty and Spunky, but he didn't gun down his accomplice.

"Why do *you* want me?" Steve asked, turning the tables.

"I keep thinking about that crazy stunt you pulled. Chasing me. Diving into the channel. You've got principles and you're tough. You're the kind of guy I want on my side." Nash paused a moment. From somewhere inside the bowels of the jail, a piercing wail could be heard. "Your turn, Solomon. You've been doing nothing but trashing me and my cause. What are *you* doing here?"

"I figured anybody who pisses off Ray Pincher can't be all bad."

Nash laughed. "It's my father Uncle Ray really hates. Clifford Nash."

He said it as if Steve should know the name.

"Dad's a professor at FSU. Geopolitics. The global

corporate conspiracy. How the military-industrial complex has taken over the country and people like Uncle Ray are just banal servants of evil, the Adolph Eichmanns of our time."

"Family reunions must be a lot of fun."

"Know what really torques Uncle Ray? My old man's white. Not bad enough he's an old lefty and a hippie pothead, but white, too. Now, here's the weird thing. Dad *thinks* black. He hung with Huey Newton and Eldridge Cleaver. When I was a kid, one year at Thanksgiving dinner my old man says he's more black than Uncle Ray. Man, they got in a huge fight over that. Ray called Dad an 'ivory tower pinko' and Dad called him a 'house nigger.' They started pushing and shoving and the turkey ended up on the floor. That pretty much ended the relationship."

Nash was quiet a moment. Maybe thinking about his father and uncle tossing the gravy boat at each other. Then he began telling Steve what happened the night before. The other Jet Skier—the one who got away with the dolphins—was Nash's girlfriend.

Oh. A woman.

Steve hadn't realized that. In the dark, a hundred yards away, in a black wet suit, there'd been no way to tell. Her name, it turned out, was Passion Conner. Steve gave Nash some shit over that, like maybe she'd plucked the name off a daytime soap or out of a James Bond book. It had a Pussy Galore or Mary Goodnight ring to it.

"Where is she now?" Steve asked.

Nash shrugged. "I tried calling her cell phone from in here. Disconnected."

That was fast, Steve thought. Either Ms. Passion Conner figured Nash would phone from jail, where calls are monitored, or the lady wanted to cut all ties with him. Smart, either way.

"What can you tell me about her?" Steve said.

"Master's in Marine Biology from Rosenstiel. Last summer, when everyone else was interning at NOAA, Passion crewed on a tuna boat. Used a hidden camera to get video of dolphins being illegally netted. Hundreds at a time, dragged under and drowned. If the crew had caught her, there's no telling what they'd have done to her. How could I not love a woman like that?"

"Was she already your girlfriend? Before last summer?"

Nash shook his head. "She looked me up when she got back to Miami. Passion heard about my work. She wanted to join ALM."

"So the two of you got all hot and bothered about the dolphins in the sea and the hamsters in the labs and decided to do something about it as soon as you fucked each other's brains out."

"Don't make it sound frivolous! It wasn't. Passion's more radical than I am."

"What about the dead guy? Cops found his rental car in a lot at the marina. ID'ed him as one Charles Sanders, Colorado driver's license."

"We met about two months ago at a bar in Islamorada. Sanders tracked me down through mutual friends in the Animal Liberation Movement."

"You seem to meet a lot of people that way."

"Sanders had done his homework. He knew about me trying to sink that whaling ship. And how I'd torn down those hunting platforms in the Glades and paint-bombed that fur store in New York."

"You're a one-man demolition team."

Nash seemed to take this as a compliment. "Yeah, I got some props in the brotherhood."

The brotherhood of anarchistic fuckups, Steve figured.

Sanders had claimed credit for some missions of his own, Nash said. Burning down a canine toxicology lab on the West Coast, a place that drugged puppies for pharmaceutical research. That was a pretty big deal in the ALM. But before he'd shown up, Nash and his cronies had never heard of the guy. Smelled cop or FBI informant. Then Sanders proved his worth. They'd broken into the primate research lab in Marathon, freeing the monkeys and setting them loose in the Glades. Except for the unfortunate ones that got turned into roadkill on Overseas Highway.

"Did Passion know Sanders any better than you did?"

Nash shook his head. "We met him at the same time."

"You mean, that's what she told you."

"What are you getting at? You think Passion knew Sanders and lied about it?"

"How should I know? She's your girlfriend."

"You're way off, Solomon. Passion loves me."

"And she shows that how? By disappearing?"

Nash had no answer, so Steve moved on. "What was Sanders doing when he wasn't saving the world?"

"Insurance."

"You're kidding."

"He had a card. Chief adjuster for some casualty company."

"And you believed that?"

"I didn't care one way or the other. But you're right. He didn't look like an insurance adjuster. Rugged guy.

Little over six feet. Maybe two hundred pounds. Fit and ripped. A terrific swimmer, like maybe he'd competed at one time."

"How'd you three decide to knock off Cetacean Park?"

"Not my idea. I'd been looking into this chain of pet stores. Figured we'd maybe crash a pickup through their window, take the animals. But Sanders said, 'Let's go bigger.' "

"And Passion agreed with him?"

"Yeah, she did. She wants to make her mark."

Steve listened as Sanders recounted the attack on Cetacean Park. Sanders had surveilled the place. A lone security guard. Old guy who sat in a shed all night watching telenovelas on a black-and-white TV. Unarmed except for a can of Mace and a cell phone. They had their plan all worked out. Sanders was supposed to slip ashore and tie up the guard. Nash had never confronted anyone mano a mano, so he was happy to let someone else handle it. Sanders was armed, a military .45, a big-ass handgun, but it was mainly for show. But when Sanders got there, there was no old guy with a can of Mace. There was Grisby. With a shotgun.

"I don't understand Sanders getting shot," Nash said. "We'd already gotten the dolphins out of the channel. Passion was in the Bay. I was almost there, too, when you jumped me. I mean, the whole thing was *over*."

"Grisby claims he had Sanders covered with a shotgun and they were just waiting for the police, when Sanders suddenly went for his gun."

"Doesn't make sense," Nash said.

"Neither does Grisby shooting him twice. Sort of like bombing Nagasaki after hitting Hiroshima."

The pieces weren't fitting together. The key to the case was finding out what actually happened between Sanders and Grisby just before the shooting. But Nash couldn't have seen anything from the channel. Neither could Bobby from the seawall. So far, it was Grisby's word against a dead man's.

"Anything else, Gerald? Anything else I need to know?"

Nash glanced around uneasily, as if someone might be eavesdropping. "There's one thing I haven't told you. It wasn't just the three of us. We had a boat, a big-ass Bertram with a saltwater tank. It was anchored a half mile outside the gate. A two-man crew. They were supposed to bring the dolphins on board in canvas nets."

Steve didn't get it. "Once the dolphins were through the gate, why not just let them swim free in the Bay?"

"Because they might go back up the channel to the park."

Meaning the dolphins liked it there, Steve thought. Spunky and Misty probably figured they'd been comped at the Four Seasons, and then along come these yahoos who want to force them to work for their supper. "Who the hell are the two guys? And where are they now?"

Nash shrugged. "Sanders hired them. I never knew their names."

Nash finished his sorry story. When the cop cars came screaming from Virginia Key toward the park, the two guys panicked and took off in the Bertram. The dolphins swam God knows where. Passion must have headed to Crandon Park Marina, where she ditched her Jet Ski. And no word from her since.

Steve mulled it over.

Passion missing.

Sanders dead.

Two nameless guys from the boat running loose somewhere.

And Gerald Nash left alone, facing life in prison.

Steve didn't know if his client was guilty of murder, but he surely could cop a plea to stupidity in the first degree.

*Ten*

NO MORE WAYWARD BREASTS

Driving south on Dixie Highway, Victoria couldn't wait to tell Steve the news.

She'd been deputized and had a badge and gun to prove it.

Specially appointed Assistant State Attorney for the 11th Judicial Circuit, in and for Miami-Dade County, Florida.

There'd be a story in tomorrow's paper. With more to come.

It was just what Solomon & Lord needed. A high-profile trial. And a winner. Felony murder was a piece of cake for the prosecution. In most murder trials, the state must prove the defendant intended the harm. Not so in felony murder, where "strict liability" was the rule. If Gerald Nash committed a felony and Sanders died as a result, Nash is guilty even if he didn't intend to cause an injury, much less death, and even if he did not, as a matter of fact, cause the death.

Draconian, maybe. But hey, that's the law.

They'd have new cases rolling in. Big cases. They could drop some of Steve's old clients. When Steve had first told her he defended personal injury cases, he never

mentioned the lap dancers at The Beav. His arguments
on motion calendars could be so embarrassing.

*"A man who buys a lap dance assumes the risk that
he'll suffer whiplash from an enhanced and wayward
breast."*

No more wayward breasts, she decided.

State v. Nash could solve multiple problems. There'd
be a steady flow of checks. Okay, not a fortune, but
state employment would solve the current cash-flow
crunch. And when those new clients rolled in with big
retainers, her professional life with Steve would be easier, too. No more scraping up leftovers in the bargain
basement of the courthouse. No more ads on bus
benches: *Solomon & Lord. Hablamos Español.*

Now Victoria cruised south past Coral Gables and
headed toward Kendall. Her destination was Sunniland
Park, where Steve had taken Bobby for baseball practice. She felt the buzz that comes with good news and
high expectations.

She'd moved in with Steve six months earlier, not
without some doubts and fears. Her mother, Irene Lord,
known as The Queen to friends, family, and Neiman-
Marcus salesclerks, hadn't approved of Steve on many
grounds. The Queen's multicount indictment was di-
vided evenly between finances and status. Steve didn't
make enough money. He didn't belong to the Opera
Guild. He had a habit of being thrown in jail for contempt. And you'd have to mug Steve to get him to the
Sunday night seafood buffet at the country club.

At first, her mother tried to persuade Victoria not to
live with Steve. Her advice had a quaint feel to it. *"A
man won't buy the cow if he's getting the crème fraîche
for free."*

The Queen's attitude changed once Steve helped her

when a con man fleeced her out of a bundle. *"If Stephen makes you happy, dear, that's good enough for me."* That was as much of an endorsement as The Queen could muster, and it would have to do.

There'd been the problems of their different professional styles, of course. But living with Steve had been easier than Victoria expected. She had no real complaints, though she wondered why it was necessary for the TV to be tuned to ESPN twenty-four hours a day.

Steve had been caring and considerate. Bobby was positively loveable. Victoria spent as much time with the boy as possible and had clearly become a welcome substitute for his abusive mother.

So with the car radio tuned to the all-news station, and the lead story about the shooting at Cetacean Park, Victoria smiled to herself as she pulled into the parking lot of the baseball field.

Yes, these were good times. And Steve was going to be so proud of her.

SOLOMON'S LAWS

3. When arguing with a woman who is strong, intelligent, and forthright, consider using trickery, artifice, and deceit.

Eleven

LOVE THE MAN,
HATE THE GRIN

Steve wanted to punch out the fat guy in the yarmulke but figured that wouldn't help Bobby make the team.

"We don't steal bases," Yarmulke Guy said.

"What do you mean, 'we,' Rabbi?" Steve replied.

"I'm not a rabbi, Mr. Solomon, and you know that. Are you ridiculing my spirituality?"

"Heaven forbid," Steve said with as much irony as he could muster.

The Beth Am Bobcats were practicing at Sunniland Park, and Steve was desperately trying to make his point without pissing off Yarmulke Guy, the team's coach, whose real name was Ira Kreindler.

"There's no league rule against stealing bases," Steve said.

"I adhere to a Higher Authority." Kreindler looked skyward, either toward heaven or the overhead Metrorail tracks, Steve couldn't tell which.

"*God* doesn't want my nephew stealing second base?"

"We're talking ethics. Robert can advance to second if a subsequent batter earns a hit or if the defense makes an error. But stealing?" Kreindler made a *cluck-cluck*ing sound.

Kreindler ran a wholesale meat business when he wasn't fouling up the synagogue's youth baseball team. His blue-and-white trucks, *Kreindler Means Kosher*, could be seen double-parked in front of glatt delicatessens in North Miami Beach. Around his neck he wore a golden *chai* that must have been chiseled from the mother lode, heavy enough to hunch his shoulders. He had a major-league paunch hanging over his plaid Bermuda shorts, and while he might have been able to slice brisket with speed and precision, Steve doubted he could run from first to third without a pit stop.

"You know I played some college ball, Kreindler?" Steve gestured toward Dixie Highway. The University of Miami was less than five miles straight up the road.

"Of course I know. You're Last Out Solomon. You were picked off third base to end the College World Series."

Which is when Steve considered punching the guy out, before concluding it wouldn't set a good example for Bobby. "I was a lousy hitter. But I could run, and once I learned how to study the pitchers, I led the team in stolen bases."

"You stole bases because you could?" Kreindler asked.

"Of course."

"So you believe *kol de'alim gevar*. 'Might makes right.' "

"I believe in maximizing every kid's potential. I also believe in winning, and I'm not gonna apologize for it."

"Do you really think Robert's up to this sort of thing?" Kreindler said.

"Stealing bases? Sure, once I teach him."

"Playing ball. I mean, with his problems..."

"So that's it!"

"The other boys can be so cruel. Calling Robert a 'spaz.' That sort of thing."

"Then it's your job to straighten out the little punks."

"How?"

"Shake 'em by the throat. Make 'em run laps. Teach them a sense of decency."

"Surely, Mr. Solomon, you know it's more complicated than that."

"Not for a *real* coach. You've gotta kick some kosher ass, Kreindler."

They were standing on the clipped green grass of the outfield. The Bobcats were practicing their fielding, resulting in numerous ground balls trickling between spindly Jewish legs. Deep in right field, as far from harm's way as possible, Bobby picked dandelions. The boy had been moping all day. It hadn't sunk in at first, Steve thought. But when Bobby realized that Spunky and Misty were gone, that there was no way to find them, the pain tugged at his heart. Steve had hoped baseball would take Bobby's mind off his lost pals.

Ten minutes earlier, Steve had been teaching his nephew the fine points of base stealing. With a right-handed pitcher, watch his heels. If he lifts his right heel before the left, he's throwing to first. If the left heel leaves the ground first, he's throwing to the plate.

That's when the Kreindler, bald spot covered by his yarmulke, his nose smeared with sunblock, shades clipped onto his glasses, waddled over to instruct Steve on ethics.

If Steve hadn't missed the league organizational meeting, maybe he'd be the Beth Am coach. Unfortunately, he'd spent that night behind bars, in a holding cell, a little matter of ordering pizza and two six-packs of beer for a jury deliberating a DUI case. Not that

Steve minded an occasional contempt citation. One of the first things he'd told Victoria was that a lawyer who's afraid of jail is like a surgeon who's afraid of blood.

Just then, as Steve was thinking about Victoria, he caught sight of her, walking toward him along the first-base line. Long strides with those tennis player legs. She wore a green silk blouse and a white skirt and Versace shoes of white, green, and red, sort of like the Italian flag. Steve had been there when Victoria bought the shoes. She'd nearly gone for a brand called "United Nude," which the salesclerk boasted was "a sculpture, not a shoe." Both pairs looked as comfortable as walking on broken glass.

She carried a red leather handbag, a Hermès Birkin. Steve wouldn't have known a Hermès Birkin from a kosher gherkin, but Victoria seemed overjoyed when her mother gave her the bag. He didn't understand what the fuss was about until Irene Lord said it had been a gift from a French gazillionaire she'd met on the Riviera, and that the damn thing had cost fifteen thousand dollars. Steve could understand spending that much on a flat-screen, high-def TV with surround sound, but a *handbag*? There was so much about women that completely bewildered him.

Victoria waved at Bobby, who now sat, cross-legged, talking to an egret that had landed in the outfield. Steve told Kreindler they'd discuss baseball ethics later and trotted toward the woman he loved, intercepting her at the first-base bag. She tossed both arms around his neck, and they kissed. Not a *howdy, how are you* kiss. Deeper. A *wanna jump your bones* kiss.

"Wow," he said.

"I have great news."

"Hey, me, too, Vic."

"Got a new case. A big one."

"Likewise."

"That shooting at Cetacean Park," she said. "I'm going to prosecute."

"What?" He couldn't have heard her correctly.

She couldn't have said "prosecute."

They were defense lawyers. They represented the persecuted, the downtrodden, the occasionally innocent.

Prosecute? She might as well have said, "I'm going to become a prostitute."

"Pincher's conflicted out," Victoria babbled on. "I've been appointed." She reached into her ridiculously expensive handbag and flipped out a badge, embossed with a gold star. *Special Assistant State Attorney.* "The guy you caught. Gerald Nash. He's being charged with—"

"Felony murder. I know. I'm defending him."

That stopped her. But only for a second. She blinked and said, "No way, Steve."

"He retained me this morning. Without a retainer. But still, he hired me."

Victoria chewed at her lower lip. "So what are we going to do?"

"Easy. You've got to withdraw."

"Why me?"

"Because it's my case, Vic. I got there first."

At home plate, Ira Kreindler was hitting fungoes to the outfielders, or trying to, but mostly he dribbled soft grounders down the foul line.

"You're a witness," she said. "You can't represent the defendant."

"Two cops saw me grab the guy and arrested him on the spot. My testimony's not needed."

"Did you hear Nash make any statements against interest?"

"If I did, I sure as hell wouldn't tell you."

In the outfield, a pop fly headed toward Bobby, who staggered under it, waving his arms like a drunk chasing a butterfly. The ball plopped into and out of his glove, bounced off the top of his head, and dropped to the ground. Bobby rubbed his head and spun around 360 degrees, looking for the ball.

"Nice catch, spaz!" Rich Shactman yelled from center field. He was the best player on the team, a powerfully built slugger, a kid who looked like he'd been shaving since kindergarten. Steve itched to tell the punk to lay off Bobby, but part of growing up is learning how to handle bullies, so he kept quiet.

Turning back to Victoria, Steve said, "I'm gonna have to pull rank here."

"Rank?"

"I'm the senior partner."

"We're *equal* partners."

"But I've got seniority. Rank and grade. If this were the army, I'd be the general."

"If this were the army, you'd be court-martialed."

"So, tell me this: When you opened that fancy bag of yours just now, was that a gun I saw?"

"What about it?"

"Are you going all *Thelma and Louise* on me?"

"Every prosecutor gets a gun."

"You're talking like this isn't a one-case deal. Like you're planning on some permanent changes."

"Would you just relax, Steve? I'll be back as soon

as the case is over. Think of the publicity I'll get. This gives us a chance to upgrade our clientele."

"Nothing wrong with the cases I bring in."

"Really? What about Needlemeyer versus Needlemeyer? The kid suing his parents for being ugly."

"Not just being ugly. Passing on the genes."

"That's what I mean. Junk cases, when I can win a murder trial."

"You mean lose a murder trial, because if I'm defending, it's gonna be talking cockatoos all over again."

"You planning to take a dump on my sleeve?"

"Anyone who steps into court against me risks utter and total humiliation. You know that."

"Now you're *threatening* me?"

"Just telling it like it is, cupcake."

"Cupcake? You're really trying to piss me off, aren't you?"

"Why would I do that, sweetie?"

"Because you think I'll lose my cool. You think I'll say nasty things about what a bastard you are. Then I'll feel guilty and apologize. After that, I'll have no choice but to withdraw from the case and let you have your way."

"You think I'm that clever?"

"I think you're that devious. But it's not going to work."

Steve didn't reply. He grinned at her, as if he'd just filled a straight on Fifth Street, and she held nothing but a pair of cracked aces.

* * *

Love the man, hate the grin.

I *do* love him, Victoria reminded herself.

But I hate that lopsided, wiseass, gotcha! grin.

Daring her to try a case against him. Hauling out the memory of birdshit on her jacket, thinking he could intimidate her. But she saw right through him.

"You're scared, aren't you, Steve?"

"What?"

"You're scared of a powerful woman. So you've got to swing your club like some caveman."

"You've been reading Maureen Dowd again, haven't you?"

"When we go out to dinner, why do you always pay?"

"I don't. I put it on the firm credit card. You're paying half."

"But you insist on using *your* card. Why can't I put it on mine?"

"What difference does it make?"

"Are you playing dumb or are you really that obtuse?"

"Is there a third choice?"

"You maintain control by whipping out that card. MasterCard becomes your penis."

"That's your second dick metaphor in the last minute. Are you horny?"

"Ha!"

"Because you're a little flushed. Or is it that time of month?"

She took a deep breath and reminded herself, yet again, that she loved this man, no matter how aggravating he could be. "Last bastion of male chauvinism, attacking our reproductive system, as if it makes us weak. When, in fact, it's your Y chromosome that makes you the weaker sex."

"You *have* been reading Maureen Dowd."

"It's an evolutionary fact. The male chromosome is

losing genes. Men are losing their potency, but you still try to act like Genghis Khan."

"What are you saying? You want to go off the pill?"

She smiled sweetly. Then she said, "You can't stop me, Steve. I'm going to prosecute this case. And I'm going to win."

"Hit me with your best shot, Vic."

"Oh, I will. I'll chop you into little pieces and use you for bait."

"Ouch."

"But if I feed you to the sharks, they'll never touch you."

"Professional courtesy," Steve acknowledged, nodding.

"So I'll just annihilate you in the courtroom."

"How? Bore me to death?"

"I'll file memos of law on every motion, briefs on every legal issue, make you work for a change."

"Great. Death by a thousand paper cuts."

"I'll beat you in front of the jury, too. In opening. In cross. In closing. I'll tie you in knots. And I'm gonna do it in a way you never could. I'm gonna win fair and square."

Twelve

RICH (THE SHIT) SHACTMAN

Walking along the corridor at Ponce de Leon Middle School, Bobby was totally bummed. He'd never see Spunky and Misty again. By now, they could be in the outer islands. Starving. They needed to eat thirty pounds of fish a day. Would they know how to catch their own? Or would they be waiting for someone to feed them?

In some weird way, Bobby felt responsible. If he'd only reacted faster, maybe he could have saved them. He could have told the dolphins to hide. They'd have understood him. They'd have gone underwater and stayed there for twenty minutes on one breath.

Deep down, he knew it wasn't his fault, but still. . . . *Spunky and Misty trusted me, and I let them down.*

He blamed Uncle Steve, too. He'd refused to take out a boat and search for the dolphins, saying it was impossible. He reminded Bobby of the fisherman's prayer: "Oh, Lord, my boat is so small and your sea is so wide."

In his heart, Bobby knew his uncle was right. But still, Uncle Steve was the grown-up. He should have thought of something. Instead, he ended up representing that creep, Gerald Nash, the guy who'd messed up everything.

That's being disloyal to Spunky and Misty . . . and me.

* * *

Bobby headed for his locker through the gauntlet of jocks, weirdos, nerds, pretty girls, chubby girls, brainy girls, geeks, freaks, and sleeks.

Oh, shit.

Leaning against the gray bank of metal lockers, chewing gum with his mouth open, like a sea lion gobbling a mackerel, was Rich Shactman. A concrete block disguised as a human being, in a muscle shirt stretched tight across his hairy chest.

Yeah. A hairy-chested sixth grader. Thirteen years old, Rich had been held back a year, not because he was stupid—though he was—but because his even stupider father thought it would give Rich an advantage getting a college athletic scholarship.

Was Rich looking his way?

I never should have anagrammatized his name.

Bobby hadn't meant it as an insult. Last week, they'd been in the cafeteria, Shactman goofing off, squeezing one hand into his armpit, making farts as girls walked by. Pretty lame for sixth grade. But all the guys were whooping it up because the girls looked embarrassed, and let's face it, a farting sound is pretty funny, no matter how old you are. Bobby wanted to be part of the crowd.

Dumb. Why'd I open my mouth?

"Hey, Rich," Bobby had said casually, as if they were buds, "do you know the letters of your name can be rearranged to spell 'Can Charm Shit'?"

"Who you calling 'shit,' noodle neck?"

"No. What I mean is, you know, 'can charm shit.' It's like a compliment."

"Why you wanna compliment me, you little faggot?"

Bobby felt his face redden. "Because I—"

Shactman pushed his face close to Bobby. "Stay out of my grill, dude."

Bobby couldn't stand to be this close to anyone, except maybe Uncle Steve and Victoria. He felt claustrophobic, trapped. He also smelled garlic bagel on Rich's breath.

"I know all about you, Solomon." Shactman gave him a nasty little sneer. "Your mother's a ho who locked you in a dog cage. Now she's in jail somewhere, eating pussy in the shower."

"She's not in jail." Bobby staggered backward. Feeling puny and weak. He wanted to punch out Rich the Shit, hit him as hard as he could. But he knew Shactman would beat the crap out of him.

And then Bobby had turned and run.

In the week since the confrontation in the cafeteria, Shactman had been riding him hard. Bobby didn't understand it. He'd known Rich from Sunday school at Beth Am. He'd been to birthday parties at the Shactman home in Pinecrest. A sprawling McMansion with the biggest yard Bobby had ever seen. The lawn was a full-size football field with yard markers and goalposts. Behind a row of royal palms was a sandpit with a professional volleyball court. One wing of the house held a basketball court with a set of folding bleachers and an electric scoreboard. A lap pool was behind the house, along with two clay tennis courts—lighted, of course.

Why does one family need two tennis courts? Or five cars, for that matter?

Rich's father owned a chain of sporting goods stores,

which explained all the jerseys and bats and balls signed by Marlins and Dolphins and Heat players. Bobby dreaded Rich's birthday parties, which always centered around bone-crushing games of touch football and exhausting basketball games. But never swimming races, Bobby's only decent sport.

Now, walking toward his locker, feeling Rich Shactman's hard, mean eyes on him, Bobby felt his stomach tighten. A moving blob of students pushed through the corridor, oozing toward their homerooms.

"Here comes Word Boy," Shactman taunted. His posse of C-minus retards scratched their nuts and waited. "Hey, Word Boy, what's my name today?"

"Rich. Your name's Rich."

"And your name's Ass Burger Boy, right?"

Making a crack about his Asperger's syndrome. A friggin' riot.

A couple of Shactman's friends laughed. Bobby got to his locker, twirled the combination lock, and opened the door. Shactman leaned over and slammed the locker shut so fast, Bobby's fingers were nearly caught. "Hey! Jeez!"

"Listen up, loser. I want you off my team."

"Why?"

"Because you're a total spaz. You can't hit. You can't catch. You can't throw. I want you to quit."

"It's only a Sunday school league."

"*Only?* Where do you think the high school coaches recruit? I'm gonna play at Gulliver or Ransom, then at U of M, and I don't want a dweeb like you messing me up."

"I'm not quitting."

"You will after I shove a bat up your ass."

Bobby considered mentioning just how homo that

sounded but thought better of it. He reopened his locker, pulled out his Social Studies book, closed the locker, spun the lock, and repeated, "I'm not quitting, Rich. You can't make me."

"I know where you live, Solomon. You and your loser uncle." He turned toward his posse. "The losers live in the South Grove near Little Africa."

Bobby had never heard it called that, but yes, Kumquat Avenue was a few blocks away from the heart of the African-American section of Coconut Grove. He tried to think of a comeback, some socially conscious remark, but it would sound so lame, he just gave up.

"They don't even have a swimming pool." Shactman barked a laugh. "Where do you swim, the public pool? Ever catch scabies?"

Bobby thought about saying that, yes, sometimes he swam at the Venetian pool in Coral Gables, and sometimes he swam with the dolphins, but that would've only provoked more abuse. When confronted with ignorance, prejudice, and big muscles, the best thing to do is keep quiet. That's what Uncle Steve always said.

"Know what else I heard? Word Boy here talks to fish." Shactman poked Bobby in the chest. "C'mon, loser. Say something in fish talk."

Bobby wanted to say: *"Dolphins aren't fish. They're mammals. And I've never met a dolphin as stupid as you."*

But he didn't say that. Bobby didn't say anything. He walked away, deciding just how he was going to kill Rich (The Shit) Shactman.

SOLOMON'S LAWS

4. A prosecutor's job is to build a brick wall around her case. A defense lawyer's job is to tear down the wall, or at least to paint graffiti on the damn thing.

Thirteen

A CRACK IN THE BRICK WALL

Steve wanted his father's help on the Nash case, but instead, he was getting a tongue-lashing.

"Don't be a damn fool," Herbert Solomon drawled. "You can't try a case against your lady."

"Dad, I'm not asking *whether* to take the case. I'm asking how to win it."

"You're plowing too close to the cotton, son."

"Drop the cornpone, okay?" Steve pounded a baseball into the pocket of Bobby's new glove, trying to soften the leather. "I'm not one of your drinking buddies at Alabama Jack's."

"Son, you got two conflicts of interest. If you lose, your client will claim ineffective assistance of counsel because your judgment was compromised. And win or lose, you're risking your relationship with that fine woman."

Wearing paint-stained canvas shorts, Herbert stood at Steve's kitchen counter, dropping ice into a tumbler. Four cubes. Just like Sinatra. Then he poured his Jack Daniel's, three fingers' worth—if they were Shaquille O'Neal's fingers. The old man's face was sunbaked, and his long silver hair was combed straight back and flipped up at the neck. To Steve, his Savannah-born father looked like a Confederate general, albeit a Jewish one. Herbert still spoke in imperative sentences, a remnant of his days as a Florida trial judge.

"You best let Victoria prosecute the case, son, and you stay the hell out of it. Don't you blow it with this gal, because frankly, she could do a helluva lot better than you."

"Thanks for the support, Dad." Steve tied the baseball into the glove with a length of twine. With a deeper, softer pocket, maybe Bobby wouldn't drop all those lazy pop-ups.

"Ease up on the reins, son. Victoria's got a chance to make a name for herself, so let her do it."

"What about me?"

"You've had your shot."

"Hey, my career's not over. I'm still young, as lawyers go."

"All Ah'm saying, put your relationship first and be supportive of your gal."

"You been watching *Dr. Phil,* because you've never said anything like that, and you sure as hell weren't supportive of Mom."

"Bullfeathers! Ah worshiped your mother and Ah adored mah kids."

"You weren't there for any of us, Dad. Every night, clients, or Bar Association dinners, or judicial conferences. Always on the make, always polishing your own plaques. I wish I had ten bucks for every ball game and graduation you missed."

"Aw, don't be such a grumble guts." Herbert raised the tumbler and drained half the Jack. "Ah was a good father to you and your worthless sister."

"You ever put that up to a vote, you'd lose two to one."

"Family's the most important thing in the world. And spending time with family is priceless."

"Where's this coming from? You been stealing Hallmark cards from the Rexall?"

"Ah mean it, Stephen. You and Bobby are mah life now. You're what Ah live for."

"Really? Bobby's got a baseball game Sunday. You wanna come?"

"Sunday?" Herbert took a sip to think about it. Steve waited. It turned into a three-sip wait. "Nah. Ah'm caulking the boat Sunday."

"Uh-huh."

"Besides, why's the boy want me hanging around?"

"No good reason. Except he loves you, Dad."

Herbert could have said, *"I love the boy, too."* Instead, he drained his sour mash whiskey. With Herbert Solomon as a role model, Steve thought, it was a wonder he could express any emotions at all. Other than anger, that is.

Herbert poured himself more Jack and swirled his glass, the ice cubes *clink*ing like chattering teeth. "If that's it, Ah'm gonna sack out on the sofa and watch some pay-per-view titties on cable."

"Be my guest. I just thought you might have a tip or two on defending a felony murder trial."

"No way to defend it. It's the one charge that's stacked in favor of the state, and you know it."

"But Dad, with all your experience—"

"You got any theory of the case?" Herbert interrupted. "You got a theme?"

Better, Steve thought, the old buzzard was getting interested. "Not yet."

"Those ink-stained wretches been calling you?"

"*Herald, Sun-Sentinel* left messages yesterday. *Palm Beach Post* this morning. Lisa Petrillo from Channel 10's been camped out at my office."

"Thought she did entertainment news."

"Since you left the bench, Dad, that's what murder trials have become."

"Well, before you say anything, make sure you get your theory of the case and your theme. Then keep pounding 'em. And stay on message."

Herbert Solomon might no longer be a lawyer—he'd resigned the bench and the Bar rather than face a bribery investigation—but his mind was still sharp. As a lawyer and a judge, he was usually the smartest person in the courtroom, and well aware of it.

"Not that it's gonna be easy," Herbert continued. "From what Ah hear, your case is a loser. An open-and-shut conviction."

Steve dropped his voice into a gravelly imitation of his father. "Ain't no case open and shut till the jurors open that door and the foreman shuts his mouth."

"At least you been listening. But you gotta have something to go on. A crack in the brick wall."

Another of his old man's expressions. Before he'd been Chief Judge of the Circuit, Herbert T. Solomon, Esq., had been a terrific trial lawyer. He used to say that the prosecution's job was to build a brick wall. Strong and sturdy, brick after brick, smoothing the mortar, making it all neat and tidy. The defense didn't have to build a wall of its own. It just had to scratch away at the state's wall, searching for weak spots. Rotten bricks or weak mortar, that's what the defense is after.

Make an iddy-biddy crack in that wall, just enough

for a handhold, and you can tear the whole damn thing down.

Right. But sometimes you were lucky just to spray paint some graffiti on that old wall.

"So what do you have?" Herbert asked.

"The state's time line is fuzzy. Sanders was there three or four minutes before Grisby shot him. What the hell was going on all that time? Why would Sanders go for his gun when Grisby held a shotgun on him? And why'd Grisby shoot him twice?"

"Why was Grisby there at all?"

"He says he expected trouble after Pincher warned him about the ALM. But why be alone? Why not hire a new security guard? Or two or three?"

"You suggesting Grisby didn't want witnesses?"

"Just asking questions, Dad, the way you taught me."

"The guard that supposedly quit. He back up Grisby's story?"

"Can't find him. Moved without notifying his land-lord. I can't find my client's girlfriend, either. She was also his accomplice. Moved out of her apartment and hasn't called Nash. Then there's the victim. Charles Sanders, last known address, Denver."

"For your sake, Ah'm hoping he's got a long rap sheet."

Steve knew what his father was thinking. When defending a murder charge, it's always helpful if the victim was a lowlife who wouldn't be missed by law-abiding, God-fearing citizens like the dozen good folks in the jury box.

"No priors," Steve said. "Military. Retired Navy. Lieutenant Commander in the SEALs."

"Jesus, Mary, and Joseph. Next you're gonna tell me he's a war hero."

"Bronze Star for defusing mines in the Persian Gulf during the first Gulf War."

"Holy shit. And since then?"

Steve shrugged. "All I know is he was stationed in San Diego when his retirement papers came through."

"What were his duties?"

"The Navy's classified everything after Desert Storm."

Herbert polished off his drink. "Don't fit. A decorated naval officer hanging out with these animal weirdos." He reached for the Jack Daniel's bottle. "That brick wall ain't crumbling yet, but the mortar's a little sloppy around the edges."

"That's what I was thinking."

"Jesus, Ah like a good puzzle."

Deep into it now. Steve watched his father, his crinkled eyes seemingly focused on a distant horizon.

"So what do you think, Dad?"

"Tough cases are more fun, and this one's a doozy. If only you could stay in the damn thing."

"Keep going."

"Can you get your client to waive the conflict?"

"Absolutely. He wants me."

"Can you keep things peaceful with Victoria?"

"I can try."

"Then go for it. But keep focused, son. It's State versus Nash. Don't make it Solomon versus Lord."

Fourteen

WHAT'S A MOTHER FOR?

Victoria wanted her mother's advice.

How can I beat Steve in the Nash case and still preserve our relationship?

But, as usual, Irene Lord, aka The Queen, was wrapped up in her own melodrama. "I've never been so humiliated," she huffed. "My daughter's paramour suing *me*."

"Mother, no one's had a paramour since Barbara Stanwyck was making movies."

"Your live-in lover, then." Irene sniffed, as if she found the notion of cohabitation distasteful.

The air was tinged with rosemary, eucalyptus . . . and malice. Mother and daughter were settled into comfy chairs at the Bal Harbour Spa for their monthly pedicures. Irene wore a purple Hervé Leroux bandage dress with a matching boomerang clutch. Her shoes—until she'd ditched them for her pedicure—were rainbow-colored Cavalli slingbacks with a heel just shy of four inches. Her hair—the color of champagne—was swept up, revealing her graceful and still taut neck. Over the years, many men had told

Irene that she looked like Princess Grace of Monaco, and she never disagreed.

"Suing me is just so tacky," she said as Ileana, the spa attendant, patted her feet dry.

"Steve didn't sue you, Mother. He sued your country club. You just happened to be chairperson of the membership committee, so you were named in your representative capacity."

Irene dismissed that notion with a wave of her freshly painted fingernails. "My name's on the papers."

"A technicality."

"Tell that to Gloria Tuttle and Helen Flagler."

Gloria and Helen. Her mother's best friends. The royal bitches of the Biscayne Royale Country Club. Steve had sued the club on behalf of a client who'd been expelled after his conviction for mail fraud. Something about violating the high-moral-character clause of the membership agreement. Steve's lawsuit claimed that his client was being unfairly singled out, given that a sizeable percentage of his fellow Royale members were philanderers, tax cheats, and alcoholics. He threatened to question every member, under oath, in open court.

"Ouch! Jesus, Ileana."

"*Disculpe, señora.*" Ileana dropped her orangewood stick. "*Lo siento.*"

"You know how sensitive my cuticles are."

Victoria had come today not only for the pedicure but to seek her mother's counsel. The problem, as always, was to get The Queen to focus on someone other than herself. If self-absorption were an Olympic sport, Irene Lord would win the gold.

Ileana was rounding the corners of Irene's little toe with a grit board when Victoria finally pleaded,

"Mother, I need your full attention, and I really need your help."

Irene raised her plucked eyebrows—dyed to match her hair—and smiled tolerantly. "Of course. What's a mother for?"

It took Victoria fifteen minutes to describe the conflicts of interest, both professional and personal, plaguing her. Then, as Ileana finished up with a delicious calf massage, The Queen weighed in. "You're in a lose-lose situation. If you win the case, you'll lose Steve."

"Why?"

"Men are fragile creatures with tender egos, dear. Let's say you're having dinner. If you mention that your man is losing his hair, he'll never get it up that night."

"Steve's not losing his hair. Or his erection."

"Not yet. But if you beat him in court, what then?"

"Steve's ego is fine. He never hogs the spotlight when we try cases together. He always gives me credit when we win."

"Sure, when you're on the same side."

"What about when I beat him in tennis? He just laughs it off."

"Because tennis is *your* game. You were the college player. He's just a hacker. But the courtroom belongs to him. It's his identity. It's where he keeps his *cojones.*"

Victoria thought about it while Ileana massaged her mother's toes, pulling each one as if milking a cow. It wasn't fair. Prosecuting a high-profile murder case was a huge opportunity. And just why was her mother so concerned about Steve, anyway?

"Why are you worried about my losing Steve when you dislike him so much?" she asked.

"My feelings for Stephen are quite irrelevant. *You* love him. And he adores you."

"So you're actually thinking of *me*?"

"What's so unusual about that?"

That's when Victoria decided. It was simple, really. Her mother was dishing out advice from a prior generation. Maybe the generation before that. The Queen was stuck in a time warp of her own mother's making. Women nowadays didn't have to defer to their mates. They no longer had to be subservient. Or worry about hurting delicate feelings.

"Mother, I am not going to back off."

Irene exhaled a breath that stopped just short of a sigh. "As long as you know the risk."

"There might be another way."

"How?"

Victoria slipped a foot into a terry cloth sandal. "I have to get back to the office, Mother."

"What's your hurry?"

"I have a motion and a brief to write. Something that will catch Steve by total surprise."

"Tell me, dear. I love surprises."

"I'm not going to beat Steve at trial. I'm going to beat him now, before we ever get to the courtroom."

Fifteen

FOOTBALL AND MURDER

Victoria was having second thoughts about her outfit. Usually, she went for a subdued and professional look. Classy and conservative.

Not St. John Conservative. More like Calvin Klein Conservative. Something in muted tweed, a one-button jacket over a knee-length skirt.

But today was different. Today she was up against the craftiest opponent she would ever face—her lover and partner.

Victoria had filed a motion to disqualify Steve as defense counsel. He was, after all, a witness to the crime. Further, it was unseemly, if not downright unethical, that the prosecutor and defense lawyer were law partners and lovers.

Stapled to Victoria's motion was a twenty-two-page well-reasoned brief, citing several dozen cases as precedent. There was no question, no gray area, no room for debate. Steve would have to step aside.

As usual, Steve the Shark filed no written response to the motion. He would rely on his verbal skills, his ability to tap-dance around land mines.

In ten minutes, they would argue the motion before

Judge Gridley, and Victoria was confident that before the morning was over, Steve would be tossed from the courtroom like an obnoxious drunk from a tavern.

At the moment, her only worries were sartorial.

She walked into Judge Gridley's chambers wearing a fiery orange tank top covered by a blue Ellen Tracy shirt jacket. The Armani skirt matched the top, and her Hermès portfolio bag matched the jacket.

Radiant orange and brilliant blue. University of Florida colors. All because *State v. Nash* had fallen into the division of Judge Erwin Gridley, Bull Gator Emeritus, one of the biggest and baddest reptiles in the state.

She had resorted to the cheap ploy only after watching Steve get dressed earlier that morning. Blue blazer, orange shirt, and that stupid tie crawling with alligators. Shameless. So she had no choice. After he'd left the house for an early hearing, she'd carefully chosen her own outfit.

As she entered chambers, Judge Gridley was nowhere to be seen. The walls displayed the usual plaques and photos; the credenza held an assortment of footballs, helmets, jerseys, and the latest national championship replica trophy. A stuffed alligator head, showing a toothy smile, sat on His Honor's desk.

Steve was already seated at the conference table, displaying his own snarky grin. "You look like a highway barricade," he said in greeting.

"And you're a complete phony. A Miami grad wearing Gator colors."

Judge Gridley rumbled in, shed his black robe, revealing orange-and-blue suspenders. Bulky, bald, and trifocaled, he plopped into his high-back chair.

Steve immediately began humming "We Are the Boys from Old Florida."

"What the heck are you two lovebirds doing on opposite sides of the table?" the judge asked in his Panhandle accent.

"Motion to disqualify Mr. Solomon as defense counsel," Victoria said. She told the judge about her appointment as special prosecutor, her relationship with Steve, and his presence at the crime scene. She cited three appellate court cases in support of her position, and spoke with the confidence of a lawyer who is both factually prepared and legally correct.

As she laid out her argument, the judge fiddled with a flatbed railroad car. Not a real one, a Lionel model. Gridley's obsession with his alma mater was nearly matched by his love of model trains. A three-inch O-gauge track ran from the desk, around the conference table, and back to his desk again. Lawyers took care not to place their pleadings on the tracks in order to avoid derailments.

Victoria finished her argument, and leaned back in her chair. Judge Gridley turned to Steve. "Ms. Lord's got more horsepower than the Sunset Limited. I'm inclined to toss you off the train unless you can get me to switch tracks, Counselor."

"A defendant is entitled to counsel of his choice," Steve began. "I've been retained by Gerald Nash. Obviously, this situation is delicate because the prosecutor is both my law partner and..."

He paused, apparently searching for a word.

And what, smooth talker?

"Playmate," he concluded.

Victoria bristled. "I'm no one's playmate, Your Honor. Mr. Solomon and I live together. Currently."

"If y'all are shacked up, Mr. Solomon, how you gonna try a case against each other?"

"Precisely, Your Honor," Victoria said. "The only question is, whom shall Your Honor require to withdraw?"

"Yes, *whom*?" Steve echoed in his smart-aleck tone.

"Mr. Solomon must withdraw. He was present at the crime scene and apprehended Gerald Nash," Victoria said. "He's a witness."

Steve loosened the knot on his alligator tie. "A witness to an uncontradicted fact. My nephew saw Mr. Nash. So did Wade Grisby. So did the cops."

"Irrelevant, Your Honor. Mr. Solomon can't be both a witness and defense counsel."

"Bogus argument, Judge. We'll stipulate to my client's presence at the scene."

"Don't call my arguments bogus," Victoria snapped.

"Bogus, bogus. Hocus-pocus."

You can't taunt me into losing my cool. Not anymore.

"Your Honor," Victoria said, calmly, "the case of State versus Linsenmeyer settled this issue. I've prepared a brief on the point."

"Lemme see it." Gridley grabbed his long-billed engineer's hat and yelled, "All a-b-b-b-board!" He hit a switch on a console, and a model train started chugging from his desk to the conference table. A classic engine, the Florida East Coast Railway Warbonnet, a scale model of the diesel that a half century ago transported the Gator football team to Jacksonville for the annual game against Georgia.

The train pulled to a stop in front of Victoria, who placed her memorandum on a flatbed car. The whistle tooted, white smoke billowed from a tiny stack, and the train *clickety-clack*ed to the end of the table, where it passed through a tunnel.

"You got a countermemo?" the judge asked Steve as the train emerged from the tunnel and made a slow turn in his direction.

"No, sir. I rely on common sense, the Common Law, and Your Honor's own uncommon wisdom." Now he was humming the fight song, "The Orange and the Blue."

The Warbonnet sped past Steve, tooting twice, spewing a trickle of smoke.

When the train pulled to a stop, the judge grabbed the document, scanned it, and said, "Ms. Lord is right on the law. I'm sorry, Mr. Solomon, but without some contrary precedent, the conductor's gonna have to toss you off the train somewhere around Ocala."

"Judge, just because I didn't brief the point doesn't mean I don't have precedent. I'd cite the case of Florida State versus Clemson."

What case? What damn case is that?

"Also Florida State versus Auburn."

What the hell is Steve talking about?

The judge cocked his head and murmured a soft *"Hmmm."* He picked up a miniature brush and dusted off a freight car. "Bobby and Tommy and Terry. Hadn't thought of that."

Bobby and Tommy and Terry?

"When those sumbitches play," the judge continued, "you got father against sons. You get it, Ms. Lord?"

"Not exactly, Your Honor."

"Bobby Bowden coaches those dog-ass Seminoles, known in these parts as the Criminoles. His son Tommy coaches Clemson and son Terry used to coach Auburn. If a father and son can coach against each other, why

the heck can't you two oppose each other in court?"
Judicial wisdom glittered in His Honor's eye.

"But a football game isn't a murder trial," Victoria
protested.

"Damn right. Football's *bigger*. This courthouse
sees hundreds of murder trials a year. But something
like Florida State versus Clemson...well, that only
happens once a year."

Victoria was floundering. She didn't know how to
respond. There didn't seem to be case law to refute the
notion that college football is more important than
felony murder. On the other side of the table, Steve kept
quiet, not even trying to suppress that infuriating grin.

"But let me ask you this," the judge mused. "You
two aren't gonna be playing footsie under the table,
are you?"

"Certainly not," Victoria said.

"Not till after court," Steve said.

"Y'all argue when you're on the same side of the
table. I don't see much chance of collusion, so I'm inclined to let you have a go at each other. State's motion
to disqualify is hereby denied."

*Oh, no. This judge clearly played football too long
without a helmet.*

"But, Your Honor," Victoria said, "lawyers have to
go for the kill. Crush the opposition. When you're in a
relationship, how can you be expected to—"

"That train's left the station." The judge hit a switch
and the train's whistle *toot*ed. "You two are gonna try
this case. Now git, both of you. Go home and figure
it out."

"Figure what out?" Victoria said, bewildered.

"How to litigate by day and copulate by night," the
judge replied, hitting the whistle for one long, last *toot*.

Sixteen

SQUID PRO QUO

His ball cap pulled low over his eyes to shade the sun, Bobby stood in right field, legs crossed, gloved hand brushing a mosquito from his neck. He watched his own elongated shadow stretch toward the outfield fence and tried to figure the exact angle of the sun. If he knew that number, he could compute the length of his shadow within ten centimeters.

His mind drifted. He wasn't thinking about the pitcher or the batter or the consequences of a fly ball floating his way. He was thinking about the wad of bubble gum in his mouth that had lost its flavor, about the yellow jackets buzzing around the wildflowers, and about Rich Shactman.

What's the best way to kill The Shit?

Poison?

The Beth Am Bobcats were ahead 9 to 6, no thanks to Bobby. He'd struck out twice and dribbled a feeble ground ball to the first baseman his last time up. So far, no one on the Plymouth Church Pioneers had hit a fly ball to right field.

One of the hexacyanides? Pour it in Shactman's Coke.

The prick had clobbered two home runs, strutting across home plate each time, posing, chest thrust forward, as his father shot video.

Plastique? Blow him to kingdom come.

Bottom of the seventh inning, the last inning in the Palmetto Sunday School League. Bobby vaguely knew there were two outs. The game would be over any moment, and he could get out of the sun.

Speargun? Grandpop shoots Florida lobsters... when the Marine Patrol isn't around.

Bobby wondered what was taking so long. Now he noticed the bases were loaded with Pioneers. He heard the *clunk* of metal bat hitting leather ball. He looked up.

Oh, shit.

Short fly ball over the second baseman's head, into right field. Bobby took off, a flurry of elbows and knees. He wished he could run like Uncle Steve, smooth and fast.

"Catch it, dickwad!" Rich Shactman screamed from center field.

The ball reached its apogee; it started its descent. Bobby's brain crackled.

Catch the ball and the game's over.

If it drops in front of me, it's only a single. One run scores; maybe two. We're still ahead by a run.

Or I could dive and make the catch.

On *Sports Center,* they always show those diving catches on the Top Ten plays. Major leaguers make it look easy. Slide on your rump; reach out; grab the ball underhanded just above the grass; hoist the glove to show the ump you caught it clean.

Go for it!

Bobby tried to slide, but his legs tangled and he

tumbled forward, arms spread, as if he'd been shot in the back. A second later, he felt a thump as the ball bounced off his butt and landed in the grass.

"Pick it up, dipshit!"

Shactman again, louder. Running toward Bobby, maybe to pummel him, maybe to grab the ball himself.

The runner from third walked home.

Bobby scrambled to his feet, whirled, located the ball just behind him.

The runner from second scored standing up.

Bobby picked up the ball, but for reasons known only to the gods of the game, he dropped it. Picked it up again, dropped it again. Shactman was shrieking.

The runner from first crossed the plate. The score was tied.

Bobby picked up the ball cleanly this time. The batter neared third base at full speed. The third base coach waved him around, betting Bobby couldn't make a decent throw to the plate.

Plenty of time. I can do this.

Miguel Juarez, the husky catcher, a ringer on the Beth Am team, stood at the plate, waiting for the throw.

I can throw the ball to him on the fly. Yes, I can.

The batter rounded third, head down, hauling ass for home. Bobby remembered everything Uncle Steve had taught him. He planted his back foot and stepped forward, reaching down with his right arm and extending his left arm for balance. He kept his eyes on Miguel and came over the top, releasing the ball just after his arm passed over his head. The motion was smooth, and Bobby was amazed at how hard he'd thrown the ball.

"A cannon for an arm." That's what they say on Sports Center *about Vladimir Guerrero.*

The throw was right on line. Straight at Miguel Juarez, guarding home plate. This was gonna be AMAZING.

"What a throw by Bobby Solomon! Our top play tonight on ESPN. Does that kid have a gun or what?"

Hands on hips, Miguel looked up. Watched the ball sail over his head. Over the backstop. Over eight rows of bleachers. And land in the parking lot with the sound of glass shattering.

The batter scored and leapt into the arms of his ecstatic teammates. High-fiving, yelling, laughing, smacking one another on the shoulder, blowing bubbles with their gum. Final score: Plymouth Church Pioneers 10, Beth Am Bobcats 9.

"Gonna mess you up, dipshit."

Rich Shactman jacked an elbow into Bobby's gut, then trotted past him toward the dugout. Bobby dropped to one knee, thinking he might vomit, but he caught his breath and got back up.

Coach Kreindler gathered the team's bats in front of the dugout.

"It's him or me, Coach!" Shactman tossed his glove against the concrete block wall of the dugout.

Kreindler turned toward the boy, confused, the aluminum bats *ping*ing against each other.

"The scouts from Gulliver and Ransom only come to the playoffs," Shactman whined, "and we'll never make them with Solomon messing up."

"Nu? What would you have me do, Rich?"

"Throw Solomon off the team. I'm your star."

"Gevalt."

"So what's it gonna be, Kreindler? Solomon or me?"

Bobby heard every word. Watched as Kreindler shot

a worried look in his direction. But the coach never answered. Just kept gathering up bats and balls.

No. *Not poison or explosives or a spear. There's
one thing I'm better at than Shactman. Swimming. I'm
going to* drown *him.*

SOLOMON'S LAWS

5. Listen to bus drivers, bailiffs, and twelve-year-old boys. Some days, they all know more than you do.

Seventeen

THE HABITS OF DOLPHINS

"That was a great throw," Steve said.

"It broke a rearview mirror in the parking lot," Bobby said.

"Hard and true, right on line to the catcher. A bit high, maybe..."

"You're just trying to make me feel better."

"The mint chocolate chip is supposed to make you feel better, kiddo. I'm here to tell you the truth. You have what they call a long arm."

Uncle and nephew were sitting at a table outside Whip 'N Dip on Sunset Drive. Bobby had barely touched his ice cream. Steve had already polished off a cone of peanut butter swirl. And sure, he was trying to cheer up the boy. But Steve meant what he'd said. The velocity of the throw had been astonishing. The skinny kid had a rubber arm.

"You should be pitching."

"Coach Kreindler will never let me."

"I'm gonna work with you on your control, teach you a few pitches. Then we'll show Kreindler what you've got."

"When will you have time? You've got that stupid trial."

Another sore point. Bobby desperately missed Spunky and Misty. And he was still pissed about Steve defending Gerald Nash.

"Everyone's entitled to a defense, kiddo, even wackos like Nash."

"He's not charged for his beliefs. He's not even charged with releasing the dolphins. He's charged with getting a guy killed."

Spoken like a true prosecutor, Steve thought.

"You care more about that bird turd than you do about Misty and Spunky," Bobby fumed.

"Not true. But there's nothing I can do about your pals."

"You could have rented a boat and looked for them."

"We've been through that, Bobby. Where would we look? The ocean's too damn big."

Bobby knew his uncle was right, but he was too upset to let up. "Your client's full of shit, you know."

"Meaning what?"

"I don't wanna talk about it."

"C'mon, kiddo. Why's Gerald Nash full of shit?"

"I'm taking the Fifth."

Steve had learned a long time ago that a trial lawyer, especially a solo practitioner, needed help. Take the Courthouse Gang, for example. Most lawyers ignored the retirees who hung around the Justice Building, wandering from courtroom to courtroom, seeking free entertainment. Hell, most lawyers never even *noticed* the oldsters.

In his first year practicing law, Steve made friends with Marvin (The Maven) Mendelsohn, Teresa Toraño, and Cadillac Johnson. All over seventy, and all had seen hundreds of trials. Together, the three were great at sizing up people, figuring out when they're lying. Maybe it takes a long life to develop those instincts. Whatever the reason, Steve relied on the Gang for picking juries. He couldn't afford a high-priced jury consultant, or even a low-priced one, for that matter. He could, however, buy The Maven a Reuben with extra Russian dressing, the standard fee for courtroom advice.

Bobby added something else to Steve's team. The kid knew everything. Okay, that was an overstatement. But thanks to his echolalia and eidetic imaging, he remembered virtually everything he'd ever seen or heard. It was a gift, one of the quirks of his central nervous system abnormalities. While Steve couldn't tell you what he ate for breakfast, Bobby could remember every license plate he'd seen on a drive from Miami to Disney World.

"Why are you holding out on me?" Steve asked.

"*No hablo Inglés.*"

"Bobby, this is your uncle Steve. We're tight, right?"

"Most definitely."

"So . . . ?"

The boy's abilities were not limited to memorization. If he grew interested in a subject—baseball, supermodels, dolphins—he was able to engage in abstract thinking, too. He could demonstrate mathematically that runs-batted-in are the least meaningful statistic in baseball. He invented a body-fat analysis that could reveal—using only photographs—which supermodels had surgically enhanced breasts. And he was translating dolphins' clicks and whistles into dozens of words and phrases—that effort interrupted by the felonious Gerald Nash.

"Why's Nash full of shit?" Steve persisted.

Bobby slurped at the ice cream puddling in his cup. "Nash told you the dead guy had a boat with a lift to pick up Spunky and Misty, put them in a tank."

"Right. They were going to take them to the Straits and let 'em go."

Bobby screwed up his face in a look that said *bull-shit*. "Why go to all that trouble?"

"Because if they left the dolphins in the Bay, they'd swim right back up the channel to the park."

"So why didn't they? The gate was wide open."

"I don't know. You tell me, kiddo."

"The only way they'd come back was if somebody trained them to."

"Okay, maybe your two pals would have just hung out in the shallows near the gate until Grisby came for them."

"No way. The water's all skanky there with oil and crud from the Crandon Marina. Spunky would have led Misty to deeper water. Then they'd get hungry and go out to open sea. They'd be free, just like your client says he wanted."

"Maybe Nash didn't know that."

"Then he didn't do his homework."

"Okay, kiddo. Spit it out. What are you saying?"

"Victoria will be pissed if I tell you."

"What? You're conspiring with the enemy?"

Bobby swirled the ice cream, now a green river with logs of floating chocolate. "I'm hoping Victoria whips your butt," he muttered.

"Thanks. You and Dad are my biggest supporters."

The boy spooned up some melted ice cream and kept quiet.

"Let's make a deal, kiddo. Only share with me what you tell Victoria. Nothing more. No special treatment."

"It isn't that much," Bobby said.

"Fine. Whatever you've got."

Bobby shrugged. "Your client didn't want to set Spunky and Misty *free*. If there was a boat to pick them up, it's because he was going to *keep* them."

Eighteen

EVERYTHING BUT THE TRUTH

Steve drove along the Miami River toward the county jail. He needed to confront Gerald Nash and get the truth. Bobby was right: the guy's story wasn't holding up. Just why did Nash need a boat to pick up Spunky and Misty? Why risk injuring them? Why slow down your own getaway? Why not just let the dolphins go *free?*

Clients lie. They lie under oath, which is bad enough. But they also lie to their own lawyers, which to Steve was both a capital offense and terminally stupid. Steve gave a speech to every lying, thieving, violent client he'd ever had:

"Lie to your priest, your spouse, and the IRS, but always tell your lawyer the truth."

It seldom worked. He didn't really expect it to. Clients lie for all sorts of reasons. Sometimes they're embarrassed at what they've done. Sometimes, if they admit guilt, they're afraid you won't fight as hard for them. That, of course, was ass-backwards. You have to fight harder for someone who actually did the deed. How else could you win?

Long ago, Steve decided there were several ways to pry the truth from perjurious clients.

You can plead with the weaselly bastards: *"Gerald, please. I can't help you if you don't tell me what really happened."*

You can treat your client like an adverse witness. Bob and weave and cross-examine: *"But Gerald, yesterday you said the moon was made of green cheese. Were you lying then or are you lying now?"*

Or you can pound them into submission with a frontal assault: *"Nash, you self-righteous prick. I know you're lying, and unless you come clean, I'm going to withdraw and let the public defender mishandle your case."*

As he walked into the county jail, Steve still hadn't decided on his approach. He figured he'd just look at Nash and instinctively know what to do.

The visitors' room was crowded with wives, girl-friends, and children of the men who were awaiting trial or had been sentenced to less than a year's incarceration. The place smelled of dried sweat, dirty feet, diapers, and machine oil. From inside, inmates shouted and wailed. Steve had come to believe that modern jails and medieval mental asylums had a lot in common.

He had been here hundreds of times, but the overweight sergeant at the desk still insisted on making him show his Florida Bar card when logging in.

"Crenshaw, why do you do this? You know me."

"I figure one day, after they disbar you, you'll show up without that card."

Sticking out his tongue at the security camera, Steve signed the sheet. He waited for Crenshaw to hit the buzzer and open the steel-barred door.

"Can you hurry up, Sergeant? I've got a wrongfully accused man waiting for me."

"Nope. Regs say I can keep out any visitor who's inappropriately dressed."

"What are you talking about?"

"Your T-shirt, asshole." He pointed at Steve's chest and the slogan: *What Would Scooby Do?*

"What's wrong with it?"

"It's blasphemous."

"It's satirical. Like that old bumper sticker *'Jesus Saves. Moses Invests.'* It's all in good fun."

"Solomon? That's a Jewish name, right?"

"Aw, jeez, Crenshaw. Don't pull a Mel Gibson on me."

"You wanna come into my house, you gotta take that shirt off. Except then you'd still be inappropriately dressed, so I guess you're shit out of luck today."

Steve could have told him to go fuck himself. Or he could have called the ACLU. Instead, he tugged the T-shirt over his head, turned it inside out, and put it back on again.

Crenshaw glared at him. "All defense lawyers are cockroaches, ain't that right, Solomon?"

"Will it speed this up if I say yes?"

"And this is the roach motel." The buzzer sounded, and the electric lock clinked open. "One day you're gonna check in, Solomon, but you ain't checking out."

* * *

Three minutes after being insulted by the bored and burned-out sergeant, Steve wagged a finger at his client. "Nash, you stupid shit! Why are you lying to me?"

The frontal assault.

"I'm not lying," Nash whined. A kid accused of swiping cookies.

"You didn't need a boat to pick up the dolphins. If you were really worried about them swimming back to the park, you could have bolted the gate on your way out."

Nash shook his head stubbornly. Jailhouse stink clung to his faded orange jumpsuit, and he looked as if he'd lost weight on jail gruel. "We were afraid they'd stay there and be recaptured. Or just swim back up the channel when the gate was opened. That's what Sanders said, anyway."

"My nephew says he's wrong."

"I dunno. Sanders knew all about dolphins. Even their Latin name. *Tursiops* something-or-other."

Then it's even worse, Steve thought. If Sanders was so damn knowledgeable, he'd lied to Nash. But why?

"Let's start at the beginning," Steve said. "Sanders offered to provide the boat, right?"

Nash nodded. "He said he could get one with a lift and a saltwater tank."

"And the two guys on the boat. Where'd they come from?"

"Dunno. Except they worked for Sanders."

"And you have no idea where I can find them?"

Nash dug a finger into one ear. It didn't make him look any smarter. "I didn't meet them until they ferried our Jet Skis over to the Key. Never asked their names and they didn't offer. Last time I saw them was when they dropped Passion and Sanders and me off."

"How about a description? What did they look like?"

"Two guys in their thirties in good shape."

"Great. I'll look for suspects at Bally's."

"Fuck, man. It was dark out. The guys wore watch caps. They never made eye contact."

"Anything? Tattoos. A limp. Three arms?"

Nash seemed to think about it. The effort slackened his lips and opened his mouth, as if he'd suffered a stroke. "One guy was real muscular, the other more wiry. And he had a scar on his forearm."

"Which arm?"

"Don't remember. And it wasn't a scar exactly. More like a chunk missing with scar tissue built up. Like a bullet might have grazed him."

"Either guy say anything?"

"Not to me."

"To Sanders, then?"

Nash shrugged again. A lazy slacker shrug. "Only thing I remember, right before we put the Jet Skis in the water, Sanders said something about the wind picking up, asked if the Gulf Stream would be rough. One of the guys told him not to worry about it."

"Were those his exact words? 'Don't worry about it'?"

"More like, 'Stop worrying. You do your job, we'll do ours.'"

"Why would you cross the Stream? If you were gonna release the dolphins, you had lots of open water without going that far."

"I never thought about it. Me and Passion weren't going along for the ride. We were gonna ditch the Jet Skis under the Rickenbacker, then pick up her car."

"So you never asked Sanders why he was going to all the trouble to gather up the dolphins, take them somewhere, and set them free again?"

"I just figured Sanders wanted to release them on the Great Bahama Bank. You know, where there's a lot of fish to eat."

"Why not just take them to Red Lobster?"

"Okay, so maybe I didn't think this through. Maybe I didn't plan it right."

"You didn't plan it at all. Sanders did. Maybe with Passion's help."

Nash looked shocked, as if he'd never thought of that, either.

"My nephew thinks you weren't setting the dolphins free. You were kidnapping them."

"No frigging way! I believe animals have certain inalienable rights. You know that."

He seemed genuinely offended and sounded believable. A believable schmuck. He'd let Sanders, someone he barely knew, take over the job. He didn't know the guys who worked for Sanders, and his own girlfriend had disappeared and never contacted him. Now Sanders was dead, and through an odd quirk in the law, Nash faced life in prison, even if he'd done nothing more violent than break a lock on a channel gate.

Nash was technically guilty of felony murder. But Steve was starting to feel sorry for him. He'd been used and didn't even know it. The guy was a lost puppy, and Steve had no leash to bring him home.

Steve wanted to find the two guys on the missing boat. He wanted to find Passion, the missing girlfriend. He wanted to find a peaceful solution for the Middle East. But right now, he had none of those things.

"You believe me, don't you, Solomon?"

"Yeah."

" 'Cause I'm telling you the truth, dammit."

"Okay, got it."

"But I'm still in big trouble, right?"

"Yeah."

"So what are we gonna do? In court, I mean?"

"Until I come up with something better, the hammer defense."

"Huh?"

"Classic legal strategy, Nash. If the law is on your side, hammer the law. If the facts are on your side, hammer the facts. If neither is on your side, hammer the table."

Nineteen

DRESS LIKE A WOMAN,
STRIKE LIKE A TIGER

Steve knows he has a weak case, Victoria thought. Why else would he file a frivolous motion seeking sanctions against the state for discovery violations? She had turned over all the evidence. She'd filed her witness and exhibit lists, and the full police reports, not just the portions containing Nash's statements, as required. She'd made witnesses available for depositions. She'd filed a notice of "similar fact evidence" that she intended to introduce involving Nash's participation in other animal liberation raids.

But Steve, in his gunslinger mode, had filed a vituperative motion. He'd accused her of "trial by ambush," of "secreting essential exculpatory evidence," of "wanton breach of the Brady rule," and other nonsense. He sought dismissal of the charges for "wholesale violation of the letter and spirit of Rule 3.220."

At least he got the rule number right.

Now Victoria walked briskly down the fourth-floor corridor of the Justice Building, the heels of her brown suede pumps *click*ing on the scarred tile. She carried a soft leather briefcase, and her quick pace made it appear she was late for court. Instead of twenty minutes early.

"A purposeful stride. Chin up."

Her favorite law professor, a woman in her seventies, had told Victoria that.

"Walk like a man, think like a woman, and strike like a tiger."

Long before she became a professor, Sylvia Massey had worked her way up to managing partner of a deep-carpet New York law firm. It had not been an easy path. When Sylvia was a young associate, she'd been called "Honey" by the head of litigation and even worse by the female secretaries, who fiercely resented her.

"Dress as if you're going to court. Not a disco."

Victoria smiled to herself as she passed a pair of female public defenders sashaying down the corridor in short skirts and blouses opened two buttons too low. One of the women wore black fishnet stockings; the other's legs were bare.

"If you want to pick up men, go to a bar. If you want to win in court, look, act, and speak like a professional."

Old school. It made sense to Victoria. Today she wore a Coeli brown plaid jacket, belted at the waist, and a matching A-line skirt that fell below the knees. She had legs long enough for the A-line and a waist flat enough for the jacket. She looked back at the two young public defenders trailing in her wake. One chewed gum with an open mouth. The other had used a mahogany lip liner the width of a highway stripe.

What's next? Bare midriffs?

Oh, Jesus. Walking toward her was one of the paralegals from the Probation Department. A Britney Spears wannabe in a red spaghetti-strap blouse that stopped three inches above her navel. Spandex black Capri pants and fuschia flip-flops that smacked the tile as she hurried toward the Probation office.

Victoria entered Judge Gridley's courtroom. Empty, except for the bailiff. Elwood Reed was snoozing in a cushioned chair at the side of the bench. He was a stooped, lean, slow-moving man who got to his feet only twice a day—once when announcing His Honor's entrance and once his exit—and would be jobless if he were not the judge's cousin by marriage.

Victoria settled at the prosecution table and opened her partitioned briefcase. She pulled out her pleadings binder, evidence folder, research files, a yellow legal pad, a paperback version of the *Florida Rules of Criminal Procedure,* and five pens of different colors.

She waited, the only sounds the bailiff snoring and the air-conditioning humming. Steve would be late, of course. He'd whip on his tie while exiting the elevator. He'd shave with the Norelco as he waltzed down the corridor. He'd say "Howdy" to cronies, debate college football with uniformed cops, compliment a judge's assistant on her new hairdo, scope out the hallways and rest rooms for any unrepresented felons who looked prosperous enough to pay a small retainer, and in general just be . . . Steve.

The door to the corridor opened.

This is a first. Steve, early?

But it wasn't her lover, partner . . . and opponent. It was State Attorney Ray Pincher, scowling. "We need to talk, Ms. Lord." He shot a look at the sleeping bailiff, then motioned toward the closed door of the jury room. "In there."

"It's not appropriate for us to discuss the case." She

sounded a little stiff, even to herself, but it was true.
Once Pincher was "conflicted out"—admitted he was
related to the defendant—he had to stay out. Lawyers
call it a "Chinese wall," a barrier to keep the person
with the conflict of interest away from the case.

"I know the rule. But I'm no fool." Pincher stepped
into the jury room and, with a slight bow, held the
door open, waiting for her to enter the interior room.

An odd feeling came over Victoria once inside. It
was a Spartan place, having twelve chairs, one table,
and no windows. Fleetingly, she wished she had heard
all the debates that had taken place in this room. What
a primer that would be for any trial lawyer.

"Hector Diaz paid me a visit this morning," Pincher
said.

The U.S. Attorney. Victoria had never met the man,
but she knew Diaz's reputation as a political oppor-
tunist.

Pincher paced at the head of the long table. "There's
an ongoing federal investigation of the Animal Liberation
Movement. Diaz wants my dumb-shit nephew to cooperate, flip on the leaders of the group, maybe bring
down the guys who hit that cruise ship."

Victoria knew about the incident. For decades,
Florida cruise lines had deposited passengers on a
remote island for day excursions. "The Castaways
Adventure, your own private, desert island," according to the brochures. The brochure didn't mention the
tortoise beds along the beach, which the tourists
would routinely trample.

One sunny day, half a dozen men and women wearing commando gear and armed with paintball guns
landed in a speedboat. Screaming "Death to tyrants"
and "Long live the turtles," they splattered dozens of

middle-aged tourists from the Midwest. Red seemed to be the predominant color, causing lots of people to think they'd actually been shot.

Chaos, of course. Six of the frightened passengers tried to swim back to the ship. One woman nearly drowned. A man had a heart attack. The paintballers were never caught.

"Diaz suggests you offer a plea," Pincher continued. "Involuntary manslaughter. Six years. Seven years. Doesn't care about the sentence. After all, the dead guy, what's his name . . . ?"

"Sanders."

"Yeah. Sanders was a lowlife, one of the bad guys."

"He was a retired naval officer," Victoria corrected him. "Got a medal in Desert Storm."

"Have any family members contacted you? Anyone claim the body?"

"No."

"So no one cares about this guy. Why should we?"

"Felony murder's a slam dunk. You said so yourself, Ray." It was the first time she'd ever called him by his first name. But he was treating her as an equal, for once, and it just felt right. "We'll have more leverage if I get the conviction, then bargain with Nash for his co-operation."

"Already suggested it to the feds. Diaz says he can't take the risk you'll lose."

"I won't lose, dammit."

"Don't take it personally. It's not about you."

"What, then?"

"You never know what a jury will do. Or wasn't that O.J. Simpson I saw on the first tee at Mel Reese the other day?"

Victoria didn't want to plead out the case. She

wanted to win it the old-fashioned way, with the reading of a verdict, the defendant slumping over, his lawyer looking like he'd taken an elbow to the Adam's apple.

His lawyer. Steve.

Damn, what's the right thing to do?

Victoria analyzed her feelings. Usually, she approached every legal issue with dispassionate logic. But now was her thinking warped by her competitiveness, her desire to beat Steve at his own game?

"All right," she said with a sigh. "If I offer the plea, will your nephew cooperate?"

Pincher smiled. "He'd be a fool not to, but then my sister raised a house full of fools."

"You think Nash has the information the feds want?"

"No idea. The ALM isn't one group. It's a bunch of disorganized cells. Losers who hook up and do one job, then go back to smoking weed. I'm betting Gerald doesn't know a hell of a lot."

"And you told this to the U.S. Attorney?"

"Of course. But he says he needs someone inside the group. For better or worse, he wants Nash."

"So is this his request? Or yours?"

"We've got four or five joint operations with the feds. They've got more manpower and equipment than we do. I need their help, so yeah, I'm asking you to do this. But I can't force you, Victoria. You know that."

Likewise, it was the first time he'd called Victoria by her first name. She had never seen Pincher so humble. So human. There was something else, too. An air of resignation.

"Do you trust the U.S. Attorney, Ray?"

Pincher shrugged. "Diaz is a careerist who wants to

run the Criminal Division of the Justice Department. He doesn't take a crap unless someone in D.C. tells him to."

"So this is coming from Washington? Why would a couple dolphin kidnappers be that big a deal?"

"Exactly what I asked Diaz. All he'd say was something about a 'parallel investigation.' Diaz thinks my nephew's tied into something bigger than animal rights. But whatever it is, he won't tell me."

Victoria sized up the situation. If she tried the case, she'd win and Gerald Nash would get twenty-five years to life. Harsh. Especially when he didn't pull the trigger and hadn't intended to harm anyone. He was basically a naive kid who'd been led astray. If she let him plead to manslaughter, it wouldn't exactly be striking like a tiger. But maybe there'd be a measure of justice in it. Surely there'd be a measure of compassion. Then there was her duty to the State Attorney's Office and Pincher's need for federal cooperation.

"I'll make the offer," she said. "But I doubt Steve will accept it."

"Why? He'd be crazy not to."

"Because he's having too much fun trying to beat me."

Twenty

STEVE SOLOMON STREET

Steve parked his Mustang near the drawbridge on the Miami River, an inky and stinky body of water that wound its way through the middle of the city to the Bay. He never used the Justice Building parking lot, where his car had a fifty-fifty chance of being broken into, what with all the presumably innocent defendants in the vicinity.

Now Steve had a three-block walk to court, where Judge Gridley would hear discovery motions. He was running late for the hearing, but no matter. It was Thursday, and Judge Gridley always called his bookie right after lunch to run through the weekend's college football games. The two o'clock calendar wouldn't start until two-thirty at the earliest.

Victoria, of course, would already be there. Planning, prepping, rehearsing. Steve liked to wing it, both because he was better when he was spontaneous, and because he was criminally lazy.

He could hear the hum of tires over the 12th Avenue drawbridge. A few blocks south, the avenue had been renamed "Ronald W. Reagan Avenue" because the former President once ate lunch at a Cuban restaurant there. A number of Miami streets had been renamed by the city and county *padres*. You could get lost if you didn't know that Southwest Eighth Street, already called "Calle Ocho" by everyone in Little Havana, had been rechristened "Pedro Luis Boitel Avenue," after an anti-Castro dissident. Another few blocks of the same street were now called "Celia Cruz Way," after the singer, and yet a third stretch was named "Carlos Arboleya Boulevard," after a local banker.

War heros and artists, Steve could understand. But a banker?

Only thing he could figure, local politicians solicit wads of cash from the financial community. Which could explain Abel Holtz Boulevard, named for a banker who went to prison for perjury.

Steve's favorite thoroughfare, however, was Southwest 16th Street, which the County Commission renamed "José Canseco Street," after the famed steroid-juiced slugger and tattletale. Steve would have been even happier if Canseco had hired him for one of his domestic violence cases, but that was not to be.

Walking along the river, Steve watched a crane hoist a white Chevy Suburban onto the deck of a rust-eaten freighter. The SUV joined half a dozen others. Recent vintage, bound for the islands. A growing business in Miami, grand theft (specific) auto. Say you're in the Dominican Republic and you want a white Chevy Suburban with coffee leather seats, a navigation system, and low mileage. Place your order, and someone in Miami will steal it for you.

Having wasted as much time as he could, and feeling the heat of the afternoon sun, Steve trekked toward the Justice Building. Behind him, he heard a fishing boat bleating its whistle at the drawbridge operator.

He walked along 13th Avenue, which had yet to be renamed Steve Solomon Street, but hey, he had his hopes. Three hundred yards from the front steps of the Justice Building, a black Lincoln pulled to the curb. The driver's tinted window unzipped, and a guy said, "You Steve Solomon?"

"Not if you're a process server."

"I can help you on the Nash case. Hop in."

The driver leaned out the window and showed the smile of someone who doesn't smile much. A pink face, as if he'd just shaved. Short blond hair turning gray. Gold's Gym wife-beater tee, massive biceps and delts, as if he'd been sharing trainers with Barry Bonds.

"Nah. My momma told me never to get into cars with strangers on steroids."

The back door flew open, and a guy leapt out. Much smaller than the driver. Jeans. Scuffed cowboy boots and a black T-shirt. Short hair, broken nose. Looked like a fighter, a middleweight maybe. He gestured toward the door. "We just need a minute of your time, Mr. Solomon."

I could run. No way Cowboy Boots can catch me. But it seems unmanly.

"Call my secretary, Cece, for an appointment. She'll forget to tell me, but drop by the office tomorrow, anytime you want."

"Cut the crap and get in, Solomon." Cowboy Boots was trying to sound tough. He was also succeeding.

"Are you nuts? Look around. Justice Building. County Jail. Sheriff's Department. A thousand cops within spitting distance. All I have to do is yell—"

Steve never saw the punch. A short right, square in the gut. Steve gasped. His knees buckled. He would have hit the ground, but Cowboy Boots grabbed him neatly by the collar of his suit jacket and shoved him into the backseat, piling in after him. Steve was still wheezing to catch his breath when the car pulled out. No shrieking tires, no crazy turns. Just a smooth acceleration past the Justice Building, where Steve's presence was expected, if not entirely desired.

The driver spoke first. "Like I said, Solomon, we can help you with the Nash case."

"No. You said, '*I* can help you.' You never mentioned Oscar de la Hoya here."

"But first, you gotta help us. You know who we are?"

"No, but I know where you're going. There's a cell with your name on it about a block away."

"That ain't funny." Cowboy Boots cuffed Steve on the head with an open palm.

Which is when Steve saw it. Red scar tissue. A chunk out of the man's arm. Just as Nash had described. But not a bullet wound. Steve had seen a nearly identical divot in another man's arm. Captain Dan, one of the best fishing guides in Islamorada. It was a shark bite.

"You're the two guys on the boat," Steve said. "You were supposed to bring the dolphins aboard. But you cut and ran when the cops showed up."

The Lincoln passed under the I-95 overpass on 20th Street. "What else did Nash tell you about us?" the driver demanded.

"Nothing. He doesn't even know your names."

"You sure about that?"

"He doesn't know if you're Mr. Blue and your pal is Mr. Pink," Steve said.

Cowboy Boots smacked Steve on the head a second time. "What the hell's *that* mean?"

"*Reservoir Dogs,*" the driver explained to his dimmer friend. "The guys pulling the heist in the movie all used colors for their names."

"So why would I be Mr. Pink?"

"Never mind." The driver turned to Steve, who felt the beginning of a headache inside one temple. "You know why we're asking this stuff, right, Solomon?"

"Because you two worked for Sanders. And because you're afraid Nash can lead the cops straight to you."

Cowboy Boots snickered. It was better than getting slugged. "He thinks Sanders was our boss."

It must have been a good joke, because both men laughed.

"Hey, Solomon," the driver said. "If you gave Nash a penny for his thoughts, you'd get back change."

More yuks. These two seemed to be quite happy kidnappers. And they didn't seem terribly upset about Sanders' death, which added to Steve's confusion. Just then he remembered something Nash had said in the jail. The night of the break-in, Sanders had asked about the Gulf Stream, worried about the size of the waves. One of these guys had replied, "You do your job, we'll do ours."

A command. Not the way you speak to your boss.

These guys didn't work for Sanders.

Sanders worked for them.

But doing what? And what were they gonna do with the dolphins?

"So what is it you want from me?" Steve asked.

"There are important people who need to know what Sanders told Nash."

"About what?"

"Where we were planning to go that night, for one thing."

That stopped Steve. These guys have nothing to do with ALM, he thought. And if Sanders worked for them, he had nothing to do with the movement, either. *This isn't about animal rights. Never was. So what the hell is it about?*

"Even if Nash told me, I couldn't tell you—"

Another open palm ricocheted off the back of Steve's skull. "Sure you could," Cowboy Boots said. "Or you'll be Mr. Brown. As in shit-in-your-pants."

"But Nash doesn't know anything. You said it yourself. He needs two hands to find his dick."

The headache dug deeper into Steve's skull. Back in college, he'd been beaned by a Tulane pitcher who took offense at batters crowding the plate. The pitch cracked Steve's batting helmet and left him seeing double. Now he was starting to feel as if he'd been hit by another pitch.

The car pulled to a stop in front of the Justice Building. Steve hadn't realized it, but they'd driven in a circle.

"He's telling the truth," the driver told his pal, before turning to Steve. "Get out."

The second Steve's feet hit the pavement, the door swung closed, and the black Lincoln pulled away. Hillsborough County plates.

"S-3-J-1 . . ."

That's all Steve could pick up before the car turned the corner. He ran a hand through his mussed hair, tucked his shirttail in, and straightened his tie. Then he bounded up the steps two at a time, heading into the Justice Building. He was late for court.

Twenty-one

STUCK ON HIS SHTICK

"I'm sure Mr. Solomon will be here any moment, Your Honor. Traffic is so heavy today."

Victoria often made excuses for Steve when they were cocounsel. Now, even on opposite sides of a case, she was still sticking up for him.

"Uh-huh." Judge Gridley, berobed, was on the bench. Victoria, with perfect posture, stood behind the prosecution table.

Some judges will hold you in contempt for being tardy. Some levy a fine, five bucks a minute, the proceeds going to the Pizza Fund for Needy Bailiffs. But Judge Gridley seemed remarkably sanguine, leafing through a tabloid tout sheet called *Lou's Surefire Picks*.

The door flew open and Steve barreled into the courtroom, looking as if he'd just been dragged through a car wash. Hair tousled, shirt sweat-stained, dark complexion tinged red around the ears. He slipped into his suit jacket and tightened the knot in his tie as he hurried through the swinging gate to the defense table.

"Good afternoon, Your Honor." He nodded toward the bench, then gave Victoria a tight smile.

"What happened to you?" Victoria asked.

"Later. Let's get this over with."

"Ah, Mr. Solomon graces us with his presence," Judge Gridley said mildly, without looking up.

Steve bowed slightly. "I apologize, Your Honor."

"One preliminary matter before we take on the defense motion." The judge closed *Lou's Surefire Picks* and looked gravely at Steve. "What's your take on Florida State at Miami this weekend?"

"I generally don't bet against the 'Canes in the Orange Bowl," Steve said.

"A wise policy," the judge allowed.

"But those national championships seem like ancient history. The line's pick 'em. I'd go with the 'Noles."

The judge grunted his approval and jotted a note on his tout sheet. "Okay, Mr. Solomon. It's your motion. Stoke your boilers."

Before Steve could open his mouth, Victoria said, "The defense motion may be moot, Your Honor. I haven't had time to discuss this with Mr. Solomon, but the state has a plea offer."

"Excellent. Always happy to clear the calendar. You two take as much time as you need, while I check out the Big Ten games."

The judge licked his thumb and began turning pages on his tout sheet.

Steve whispered to Victoria: "Two guys jumped me outside."

"What! Who?"

"Later. What's this about a plea deal?"

"Ray Pincher suggested it."

"On his own?"

"No. The U.S. Attorney asked him to do it."

"Because the feds are investigating the ALM? Or something else? A different investigation?"

"How did you know that?" Victoria demanded.

Steve exhaled a sigh that was almost visible. "Someone's playing us, Vic."

"What are you talking about?"

"The shooting's just the tip of the iceberg. The feds are involved. Pincher, too. Plus a couple guys driving a Lincoln with Hillsborough County plates. It's a big conspiracy."

"A conspiracy to do what?"

"I don't know yet, Vic. Jeez, gimme a break. I was only kidnapped a few minutes ago."

She narrowed her eyes at him suspiciously.

"It's the truth," he said. "It was a five-minute kidnapping, but still ... "

"And I'm sure you reported this vicious crime to the police."

"Not yet, but ... "

She sighed. "I just made a plea offer. Your client's in a holding cell. Don't you want to discuss it with him?"

Steve turned toward the bench. "Your Honor, negotiations are over. No plea. We're gonna try this case."

The judge sighed and refolded his tout sheet. "You sure, Mr. Solomon? Seems to me your train's on a shaky trestle."

"I'm sure, Judge."

"So be it. Let's hear your motion."

"Yes, sir." Steve whispered to Victoria, "Nice outfit today."

"Thanks."

"Where'd you get it? The Librarians' Boutique?"

"Steve, what are you doing?"

"Warming up. Taking a practice swing." He winked at her and clucked his tongue. "That belted jacket makes you look *very* buttoned-up."

"It's a court outfit. How am I supposed to look?"

"Not like a Republican senator from Kansas."

"Mr. Solomon," the judge prodded.

"Malfeasance!" Steve boomed.

"How's that, Counselor?"

"Or is it misfeasance? I can never keep them straight. The state must be punished for Ms. Lord's abuse of the discovery process. We're talking stonewalling. Cover-up. Shady deals."

"Can you be more specific, Mr. Solomon?"

"I demanded all records related to the decedent, Charles J. Sanders, Lieutenant Commander, U.S. Navy, retired. And what did opposing counsel give me? A military personnel file completely redacted. Billet—classified. Commanding officer—classified. Missions—classified. His DD-214 retirement papers—missing."

"Your Honor, we gave Mr. Solomon everything the Department of the Navy gave us. He can take his complaints to Washington."

"What about the security video?" Steve demanded. "Cetacean Park has cameras on the dock. They could show exactly what happened between Grisby and Sanders. We requested the tapes and got nothing. Zippo. Zilch. *Bupkes.*"

"Mr. Solomon knows very well that a lightning strike knocked the system out the week before the incident. The camera wasn't working."

"Shades of Richard Nixon, Judge. Erased tapes. Missing records. Hiding Brady material."

Victoria wheeled toward Steve. "Nothing's been

erased. Nothing's been hidden. If I had anything exculpatory, I'd turn it over in an instant, and you know it.
You are so infuriating—"

"Judge, would you ask Ms. Lord to address the
bench and refrain from her ad hominem attacks?"

"*My* attacks?"

"Your face is turning purple. Careful, or you'll pop
that belt."

"You're the sleaziest lawyer I've ever—"

"Slept with?"

"Damn you, Solomon," she hissed.

"There she goes again, Judge."

A shrill whistling noise pierced the courtroom. Interrupted, they wheeled toward the judge. Judge
Gridley released a switch that activated a replica of a
steam whistle. "Hit the brakes, you two. You're coming into the station."

Victoria knew the drill. One bleat of the whistle
meant "Pipe down." Two meant "Not one more
word." Three blasts and you go to the pokey for contempt.

"Any more argument, Mr. Solomon? Legal argument, that is."

"No, Your Honor. We request—nay, we demand—
that the court issue its harshest sanction. Dismiss all
charges on account of prosecutorial misconduct."

Steve sat down, and Victoria turned to the judge.
"Your Honor, I hardly know where to begin. I feel like
a dozen rats are nibbling at my feet."

"Your shoes are too tight," Steve whispered.

"Mr. Solomon hurls accusations that have no basis
in fact. He should be reprimanded and—"

"But they're nice shoes," he kept at it. "You buy
them new?"

"Save your breath, Ms. Lord. Defendant's motion for sanctions stands denied." Judge Gridley edged out of his cushioned chair and headed for the private door behind the bench, speaking as he walked. "Now, you two kiss and make up."

Steve moved to the prosecution table and leaned close. "I always follow a judge's orders."

"No you don't." Turning away, Victoria began shoving her folders back into her briefcase.

"C'mon, Vic. You know I was just doing my shtick."

"And it's always *so* amusing."

"We have different styles. Maybe that's why we get along so well."

"That must be it."

"I can tell you're a little irritated."

"And who said you were insensitive to a woman's moods?"

"There's just one thing I gotta ask."

"What?"

"Is sex tonight out?"

SOLOMON'S LAWS

6. When the testimony is too damn good, when there are no contradictions and all the potholes are filled with smooth asphalt, chances are the witness is lying.

Twenty-two

THE SECOND PUZZLE

Steve wanted to talk to Victoria, but she'd hurried out of the courtroom and disappeared.

Did she look angry?

She'd seen him in court so many times, surely she knew he was just playing a role.

She's not really pissed off, is she?

They should talk about the case, share information. Even though they were on opposite sides, weren't they both out for the same thing?

Truth. Justice. All that stuff in the books.

Victoria always railed about how trials should be less adversarial and more concerned with fair results. The criminal justice system should seek the truth, not just convictions or acquittals. Frankly, he never agreed with her, and his goal was always to win. But now, with this shitstorm called *State v. Nash,* he was willing to try something new.

He wouldn't offer to share evidence with one of Pincher's dwarves on the other side. But this was Victoria. His partner. His lover. His best friend. He wanted to think through the case with her.

C'mon, babe. Let's do some justice.

He figured her first reaction would be to stiff-arm him.

"It would be unethical, blah, blah, blah."

Now, as he drove home from the Justice Building, fighting the traffic on Dixie Highway, Steve ran through the evidence.

On the face of it, Gerald Nash appeared one hundred percent guilty of felony murder. But there was just too much that didn't make sense.

The mysterious Chuck Sanders.

Grisby in the park with a shotgun and a fuzzy story about why he shot Sanders.

Two tough guys who snatched Steve off the street and pumped him for information.

Steve remembered something his father, the cagiest trial lawyer Steve ever knew, told him years ago.

"If you come across a piece of the puzzle that just won't fit, it means there's a second puzzle where it'll fit just fine."

The first puzzle was why Grisby shot Sanders at all, much less twice. Steve had taken Grisby's deposition a few days earlier. The owner of Cetacean Park testified that his regular security guard had quit abruptly and moved away.

Q: So instead of hiring another security guard, you decided to stay up all night and do the job yourself?

A: Yes, sir.

Q: With a Remington 870, even though you'd only armed your guard with a can of Mace and a cell phone?

A: I knew about those fools attacking that monkey lab down in the Keys. Not only that,

the State Attorney had warned me I might be
next. And don't forget, I'd been hit before
when I owned a dolphin park in California.
Undersea World. That's where the damned
Animal Libbers got started.

Not just one reason for Grisby to be there, his shotgun at the ready. *Three reasons.* Each one good enough, all by itself. Add them all together and what do you get? Too much sugar in the mojito.

True stories are full of holes. Life isn't a smooth freeway across a fruited plain. Life is a winding, pot-holed road, slick with oil, and studded with broken glass. It was one of Steve's laws. If a witness' testimony is too damn good, if there are no loose ends or contradictions, chances are his story is as phony as Donald Trump's hair.

In his deposition, Grisby testified that he'd been spooked by a noise. Then he spotted Bobby on the floating platform. Telling the boy to stay put, he had walked along a path to the security shed to call Steve.

So far, all true. Bobby confirmed his end, and Steve had a clear recollection of Grisby waking him up with the phone call. But then the story got murky.

Grisby claimed he walked out of the security shed and stumbled on Sanders on the path behind the ficus hedge. Sanders had silently paddled an inflatable to the dock, his face blackened, like the Navy SEAL he'd once been. He carried tape, a coil of nautical line, and a Colt .45 automatic Grisby recognized instantly from his own time in the military. Sanders had apparently expected to find an unarmed and sleeping security guard. Instead, shotgun ready, Grisby popped out of the bushes and bellowed at Sanders to freeze.

Sanders stayed cool, told Grisby he didn't want trouble, he just wanted the dolphins to be free. Then hell broke loose.

Two Jet Skis roared up the channel, herding up the dolphins.

Grisby trained his shotgun on Sanders and ordered him to surrender his handgun and move toward the dock. Grisby wanted to take a shot at the Jet Skiers, at least scare them off. Sanders refused to move, refused to give up his gun. Just stayed put, giving his accomplices time to chase the dolphins down the channel. Grisby yelled and threatened, but the guy challenged him.

"You're not a killer, Grisby."
"Don't try me."

But Sanders did try him, according to Grisby. Sanders went for his .45. Grisby fired the shotgun, catching the man in the hip with some pellets, but only knocking him to his knees.

Q: When he was hit, Sanders dropped the gun, didn't he, Mr. Grisby?
A: I guess he did, but I can't say for sure. It was dark. I was scared. I was acting on reflex.
Q: So, with Sanders on his knees, bleeding and unarmed, this "reflex" of yours caused you to rack the slide on your shotgun?
A: Yes, sir.
Q: And still on "reflex," you aimed at Sanders' chest?
A: I suppose I did.
Q: And finally, on "reflex," you pulled the trigger and fired the shot that killed him.
A: It all happened a lot quicker than that. I

*was in fear for my life. You had to be there.
You can't sit here in a cushioned chair and
judge me.*

Not a bad answer. Righteous indignation works real
well if you don't overdo it. Grisby would do fine in
front of a jury.

Nothing in the forensics contradicted Grisby. No
way to disprove any of it. Steve shifted his thoughts to
the late Chuck Sanders. Navy SEAL. Scuba diver. Hero
in the Persian Gulf. Okay, you start with courage and
savvy, all that Special Forces stuff. No rations; he'll eat
snakes and drink piss. So, sure, he might stand up to
Grisby. Believing Grisby wouldn't shoot him, Sanders
might even have the *cojones* to walk away from an
armed and scared man. But that's different than going
for his own gun.

*Once you point your .45 at the man holding a shot-
gun, you have to fire it. You have to kill him.*

Sanders had gone to Cetacean Park to steal the dolphins. But not to kill anyone. It seemed out of charac-
ter for someone with his background and no prior
criminal record.

It was a piece of the puzzle that didn't fit.

And how about the two guys who'd jumped Steve?
They'd been on a boat just outside the channel, ready
to haul away the dolphins. But why? Where were they
taking the animals? And who the hell were the "important people" who needed to know what Sanders told
Nash?

All of which added up to one resounding, unan-
swered question: *What was really going on that night?*
Steve didn't know, and he was reasonably sure his
client was just as clueless.

Twenty-three

THROWING A CURVE

Bobby called out to Spunky and Misty. In his head. Trying to communicate telepathically. First in English, then in the clicks and whistles of dolphinese.

Well, why not? We send radio signals into deepest space, hoping some extraterrestrials will phone home. *Our* home.

Bobby had read all of Dr. John Lilly's books about dolphins. Sure, lots of scientists considered the guy a nut job, a Dr. Doolittle on acid. But weren't all pioneers vilified in one way or another?

Dr. Lilly believed that dolphins not only spoke their own language but composed music. He claimed that ancient dolphins created a society with a working government and folklore passed down through the generations. Dr. Lilly wanted to create a Cetacean Nation of whales and dolphins, recognized as an independent state by the United Nations. It didn't help the doc's standing in the scientific community that he administered LSD both to himself and the dolphins.

Bobby didn't buy everything in Dr. Lilly's bag, but some of it made sense. Bobby knew that dolphins had a moral code, that they would rescue injured or ill animals. He knew the dolphin's brain was larger than the human brain. He knew, deep in his heart, that dolphins exhibit emotion in much the same way humans do. He believed that dolphins can love and be loved. What he didn't know was whether Spunky and Misty could feel what he felt right now. Utter despair.

Do you miss me as much as I miss you?

Sitting at the desk in the corner of his bedroom, Bobby squeezed his eyes shut and transmitted his telepathic thoughts.

"Spunky. Misty. Where are you?"

No answer. But he sensed something. A buzz, an electrical connection. He wished he could interpret it.

Bobby heard a car in the driveway. Uncle Steve's Mustang pulling to a stop. It was easy to tell the growling Mustang from Victoria's little Mini Cooper, with its lawn-mower sound.

The buzz stopped in Bobby's head. There wasn't room for telepathic communication and the sound of his uncle's footsteps coming down the hall.

* * *

Steve wondered if he'd been spending enough time with Bobby. The boy's moods fluctuated wildly. First he was angry with Steve for not finding the dolphins. Maybe some guilt there, too, the kid blaming himself for not stopping the kidnapping. As if he could have done anything about it. Lately, and even more troubling, Bobby seemed to be in a state of mourning. Staying in his room, refusing to go to baseball practice. Damn few wisecracks or anagrams. Steve had been desperately trying to engage Bobby on how he felt, but the boy seemed to be repressing his emotions.

The door to Bobby's room was shut.

A closed door and a twelve-year-old boy.

Bobby could be doing his homework. Or he could be thumbing through the *Sports Illustrated* swim-suit issue, pausing over Veronica Varekova or Angela Lindvall. Pausing a long time.

He felt for the kid. Bobby was a loner. Steve had been popular all through school. An athlete. A wise guy with a ton of friends. Good for the self-confidence. It was only as an adult that he started to piss people off.

Valuing the boy's privacy, remembering his own mother breezing into his room at the least opportune times, Steve knocked on the door. "Hey, kiddo."

"Yeah."

"Okay if I come in?"

"Yeah."

Steve entered cautiously. Bobby sat in front of his computer at the desk near the window.

"You okay, kiddo?"

"Yeah."

"Everything all right at school?"

"Yeah."

Monosyllables were clearly the order of the day.

Steve decided to confront the issue head-on. "Want to talk about Spunky and Misty?"

Bobby seemed to be caught off guard. After a moment, he said, "I think they're close by."

"Really? How do you know?"

"At first, I was sure they crossed the Gulf Stream and were in the islands somewhere. But now, it's like I can sense them. They're not that far away."

Steve tried not to show his skepticism. "So, do you still want to take a boat out, go looking for them?"

"Not till they tell me exactly where they are."

"Okay, then. When they give you the word, you give me the word."

Bobby turned back to his computer.

"What's up now, kiddo? Homework?"

"I'm researching ways to kill Rich Shactman."

"Great idea." Steve believed in encouraging his nephew's creative urges.

"At first I thought about plastique. A little wad of C-4 in his electric toothbrush."

"Sounds like a plan."

"But the Shactman house has security cameras at every door."

"Of course. Good thinking."

"Then I considered poisons."

"A lot of deadly ones out there," Steve agreed.

"But the tox labs are so good these days, it's pretty risky. Now I'm thinking drowning would be best. Make it look like a swimming accident."

"I hadn't thought of that."

"I'm researching how long I gotta keep Shactman underwater."

"Three or four minutes ought to do it," Steve advised.

"You have to take bradycardia into account. The body will slow down the heart to try to save itself. Drowning takes longer than you think."

Steve wanted to sneak a peak at the monitor. He didn't believe Bobby, but it wouldn't hurt to check. Steve hoped the boy was on GirlsGoneWild.com, not something like homicide.com.

Bobby exited out of the program before Steve got close enough to see.

"What do you say we go outside and toss the ball? I'll teach you how to throw a curve."

"Coach Kreindler won't let us throw breaking pitches."

"If your elbow gets sore, we'll stop."

"You think I can really throw a curveball?"

Getting interested now, his eyes showing some spark. Steve smiled and tousled Bobby's hair. Nothing gave him more pleasure than making the kid happy. "You bet you can."

"Will it drop, too?"

"Like a dead pigeon. C'mon, let's go before it gets dark."

"Coach Kreindler will never let me pitch." The boy's mood dipped, his voice as heavy as a sack of Louisville Sluggers.

"I'll talk to Kreindler."

"What are you gonna say?"

"I'll appeal to his logic."

After I jack him up against the batting cage and suggest it's hard to eat matzo with a broken jaw.

Steve heard a car pull up to the house. Victoria. "Give me a minute, kiddo. I've got to make nice with Vic."

"Why? Did you do something stupid again, Uncle Steve?"

"I tried to get sanctions against her for unethical conduct."

"Was she? Unethical, I mean."

"Of course not."

"And you're going to try to apologize?"

"Exactly."

The boy's shoulders sagged again. "I don't think we're gonna get out of the house before dark, Uncle Steve."

SOLOMON'S LAWS

7. A shark who can't bite is nothing but a mermaid.

Twenty-four

A TALE OF TWO LOVERS

Victoria stood at the kitchen counter, uncorking a bottle of Chardonnay. Usually, she didn't touch wine until dinner. Steve didn't know if this was a good sign or a bad sign.

"Hey, Vic." He went for the *welcome home* hug, but she turned away.

Bad sign.

She poured herself a glass of wine. Didn't return his hello. Didn't offer him a glass. It was okay. He preferred beer.

"Vic, I want to talk to you about the case. I think we should be looking for those guys who jumped me today."

"*We?*"

"You. The state. You have all the resources. Those two guys hold the key to the case."

She took a sip, a big enough sip to be called a gulp. "Not to *my* case."

"Don't you want to find the truth?"

"Here's the truth: Your client committed a felony. Someone got killed in the course of the crime. Felony murder. Case closed."

"Why are you putting blinders on? You're a law enforcement official, at least temporarily."

"You want it to become permanent, Steve?"

"Ouch."

"Just what is it you want from me, other than making me look bad in front of Judge Gridley?"

"Two guys snatched me off the street. I want to file a complaint."

"Right. Your alleged kidnapping."

"*Alleged?*"

"Those stunts you pull, Steve, who knows? You want to file a complaint, go downtown tomorrow and see someone in Intake."

"The least you could do is run the plates for me. I got a partial."

"The car's probably stolen."

"There could still be a lead. Where'd they steal it? Were there any witnesses? You just never know until you look into things."

"Not my job, Steve."

"S-3-J-1. Black Lincoln. That's all I got. Hillsborough County."

"I don't want to talk about it."

"But there's a puzzle that—"

"We're on opposite sides."

"Only technically."

"Right. And you don't care about technicalities. Like the ethical canons. The codes of conduct. The statutes and procedures everyone else follows. You have no respect for the majesty of the law. The beauty of the law. The law itself."

"Okay, I can see you're a little upset. . . ."

"You're as bad as your clients. Worse, maybe. You're too undisciplined to be a lawyer. Maybe too undisciplined to be a criminal. You should have taken up another profession. Anarchist might suit you."

"Did you say, 'Antichrist'?"

Her cheeks colored to a high fever. "Dammit, Steve. You knew I wasn't withholding evidence. Why did you say those things in court?"

"I was making a record for appeal."

"A false record."

"That's called 'lawyering.'"

"It's called 'lying'!"

"A fine distinction, to be sure."

"You love it, don't you?"

"Love what?"

"Being Steve-the-Shark."

"It's my job, Vic. When I'm in court, there's gonna be blood in the water."

"Not if you play by the rules."

"A shark that can't bite is nothing but a mermaid."

"Are you calling me weak? C'mon, hit me with your best shot, tough guy. I'll play it straight and still beat you."

Steve opened the refrigerator door and hid behind it, like ducking into a doorway in a thunderstorm.

"You know what your problem is, Steve? You're immature. You're irresponsible."

"That's two problems."

"You're a child."

"And your problem is, you think the law is written in stone."

"It is, dammit! That's what makes it the law!"

Steve decided to wait it out. He grabbed a Morimoto Ale in the 22-ounce bottle. It could be a long wait.

"You can't go around making up your own code of conduct," she informed him.

"Sure you can. That's what America is all about."

"Right. *Solomon's Laws.*" Her voice churned with derision. "What's the first one, the one you told me when your damn bird crapped on my sleeve?"

" 'When the law doesn't work, work the law.' "

"Right. You *boasted* about it. Well, that's not me. I don't lie. I don't break the rules. And I don't accuse opposing counsel of acts I know to be untrue."

Steve took a long pull on the ale. It tasted of roasted buckwheat. He wondered if she was finished.

"And another thing," she said.

Nope.

"Do you remember that stupid pickup line you used on me that day?" she demanded. "The day we met?"

Steve shook his head. How the hell could he remember that? And how could she remember everything he'd ever said or done that was asinine or embarrassing, or both? On that day of infamy, they were ensconced in facing holding cells. He'd flirted with her, but how could she expect him to remember what he'd said?

"You said you'd like to *mentor* me," Victoria reminded him.

Ah, that.

"It was the best of lines," Steve said.

"It was the worst of lines. I *hate* that sexist banter. And that day, I hated you. I haven't been so furious since, not until today."

Steve had said something else in the holding cells, something he remembered well.

"Cell mates today, soul mates tomorrow."

He'd passed it off as a wisecrack. But it wasn't. From the moment he'd seen her enter the courtroom that day he'd felt something for her.

You had me, Vic. You had me from "Get lost."

"You are so damned infuriating," she said now.

"I thought that's what you liked about me."

"No, I love you in *spite* of it. But I know that when I go to sleep tonight and wake up tomorrow, you'll still be infuriating. And frankly, Steve, I'm tired of it."

She sighed and leaned against the counter. The kitchen was silent except for the whir of the refrigerator.

Steve drank a hefty portion of the ale and waited. She seemed to be finished. He waited another few seconds. Then he spoke softly:

"Do you know what you just said? That you love me. And I love you, too. I have since the day that bird crapped on your sleeve and you started crying. So I'm sorry. I got carried away today. I was way over the top. It won't happen again. With you, I mean. Other lawyers are fair game."

He moved toward her, pausing long enough to let her close the distance and meet him halfway for a makeup hug. She didn't move.

"Just give me a little room right now, Steve."

"Okay, if that's what you want, I'll . . ."

But she was already out the door.

SOLOMON'S LAWS

8. When the woman you love is angry, it's best to give her space, time, and copious quantities of wine.

Twenty-five

FLIPPER GOES TO WAR

Steve kept out of Victoria's sight for the next two hours. He gathered up ball and glove and took Bobby into the backyard, where he taught him the basics of the curveball. Then, back in the kitchen, he basted some yellowtail snapper filets in a lemon pepper sauce. Next, he tossed a salad with all of Victoria's favorite ingredients, including toasted pine nuts, which he thought tasted like tree bark.

Back outside, he undertook the manly duties of firing up the hibachi without burning down the bottlebrush tree, then grilled the fish and covered it with fresh salsa he'd made in the blender. Finally, he tossed a tablecloth over the redwood picnic table and poured ample quantities of Chardonnay for his lover, partner, and opposing counsel.

Victoria was unusually silent as they ate dinner. Steve didn't push it, didn't force the conversation. He was giving her a little time, a little space, and a lot of wine.

After they polished off the flan Steve had picked up at a bakery on Coral Way, Bobby headed inside to soak his elbow in a tub of ice because that's what Sandy

Koufax, the best Jewish pitcher of all time, did after every game.

Steve figured that the wine might have softened up Victoria, and he was ready to make nice, but she slipped into the house without so much as a "See you later." Moments later, he found her down the hall, stringing yellow crime-scene tape across the door to the study.

"What's going on?" he asked. "You doing *War of the Roses*?"

"I'm moving into the study for the duration of the trial."

"Moving? Meaning you're working in here?"

"Working. Thinking. Sleeping. The room is strictly off-limits to you."

"Whatever you say." He didn't mean to sound petulant, but that's the way it came out.

"The bedroom is yours, Steve. You can keep your files there, and I won't touch them."

"What files?"

"It's customary for lawyers to bring their work home during trials."

"Really? Why wasn't I informed?"

"Should you choose to behave like a real trial lawyer, rest assured I won't peek at your work product."

"You've already seen my work product."

Not even a smile. She just ducked under the crosshatched tape and entered the study. Steve stayed in the hall, an unhappy looky-loo. "Have I been dismissed?"

"I have work to do." She began unpacking her trial bag, laying out folders on the desk. Color-coded, alphabetically arranged, neatly labeled.

The term "anal retentive" came to Steve's mind, but he kept quiet.

A moment later, Bobby, his arm in an icy sling, slipped under the tape and went to Victoria's side.

"Hey!" Steve protested. "How come Bobby's allowed in there?"

"Don't be childish, Steve," she berated him. "Bobby, you can help me if you want."

"Cool." The boy opened a folder. "Can I see the autopsy photos?"

"No," Victoria and Steve said in unison.

But Bobby was already thumbing through the eight-by-ten glossies. "Whoa! Totally janked."

"Put that down, kiddo," Steve said from the doorway.

"Bobby, listen to your uncle," Victoria said.

"Okay, but I won't tell you what ship the dead guy was on in the Navy."

That stopped both of them. The naval records had been classified.

"What are you talking about, Bobby?" Steve said.

"Autopsy photo B-18. The word *Missouri* is tattooed on the guy's arm."

"Yeah, so maybe he likes Mizzou."

"Not the university. It's says 'Big Mo' under the tattoo. That's the USS *Missouri,* the old battleship. Its last mission was in Desert Storm in 1991."

Steve pushed his way through the yellow tape, like fending off a cobweb. "Keep talking, kiddo. I'm betting you know what the *Missouri* did in the war."

"Fired a bunch of Tomahawk missiles at the Iraqi Army."

"Anything else?"

"Shelled the shoreline, the big fake-out to make Saddam think we were invading from the sea."

"C'mon, Bobby. Don't hold out on your uncle Steve."

"Oh, you mean the dolphins."

Innocent as a twelve-year-old wise guy can be.

Victoria snatched the autopsy photos from the boy. "What about the dolphins, Bobby?"

"They're from the CIM." The kid grinned. This was his moment, and he was going to milk it.

"If you don't tell us right now, I'll never teach you the split-finger fastball," Steve threatened.

"The Cetacean Intelligence Mission. The *Missouri* transported the dolphins. Their handlers, too. Then smaller ships took them to ports in the Gulf for operations."

"What operations?" Victoria demanded.

"Clearing shipping lanes into Umm al Qasr. The dolphins spotted the mines, and then the SEALs defused them."

"Flipper goes to war," Steve muttered. "Amazing."

"Dolphins are the bomb-sniffing dogs of the ocean. They use echolocation to work in total darkness. They can dive a hundred times without rest."

"This Cetacean Intelligence *mishegoss*. Where's it headquartered?"

"The Naval Warfare Systems Center in San Diego."

"Bingo! Sanders' last stop before retirement. And that medal he got for defusing mines in the Gulf . . ."

"He had to be working with the dolphins," Bobby said, with the certainty of a boy genius.

Steve turned to Victoria with a triumphant look. "See? What did I tell you?"

"You told me you were kidnapped by two thugs. What's that have to do with dolphins in the Persian Gulf?"

"It proves Sanders was never an animal rights guy. He risked the dolphins' lives on every mission. True believers like Nash would never do that. They think it's unethical to ride horses. They hate the idea of German shepherds working with cops, of using canaries in mines. Nobody in the Animal Liberation Movement would ever risk one of his pals being turned into dolphin burger."

"Gross, Uncle Steve," Bobby said.

"Sorry. Can't you see it, Vic? Sanders knew everything about dolphins, including how to choose the smartest ones."

"Spunky and Misty," Bobby chimed in.

"The stars of the show," Steve continued. "The best-trained dolphins in the park. Maybe the best on the East Coast."

"So what was Sanders going to do with them?" Victoria asked. "And what's it have to do with the guys who grabbed you?"

"Still working on that. But when I figure it out, I'll bet all the pieces of the puzzle fit together."

"I suggest you do your figuring in a hurry," she said. "We pick a jury in the morning."

Twenty-six

ON CAT'S FEET

Victoria knew precisely what Steve was doing when she spotted him at 7:45 A.M. in the jurors' parking lot.

Lurking. Tying his shoes. Pretending to smoke a cigarette. But really spying. Checking out the bumper stickers.

"Ban Fur." Defense juror.

"My Kid Can Beat Up Your Honor Student." Prosecution juror.

She watched as Steve sidled up to car windows, peeking inside. She could practically hear his voice.

"People leave clues about themselves everywhere, including their car seats."

A wad of traffic tickets. Defense juror.

Guns & Ammo magazine. Prosecution juror.

A book by Rush Limbaugh. Simpleminded juror.

If Steve could get into trunks and glove compartments, he'd do it. Watching him, Victoria almost smiled. He made a big deal about spending so little time on trial preparation. But he prepped, all right, in his own devious and cockeyed way.

Now, just after nine A.M., Judge Gridley was perched on the bench. The spectators lounged in the gallery.

Steve manned the defense table. He'd cut his dark hair so that he no longer resembled a beach bum. In his trial uniform—a pin-striped charcoal suit, pale blue shirt, and striped tie—he almost looked like a real lawyer. Gerald Nash sat alongside, a clean yellow pad in front of him, as if he might write useful notes in his own defense. Victoria, surrounded by a picket fence of files and books, sat alone at the prosecution table.

Voir dire.

She knew every single one of Steve's tricks in picking a jury. His strengths, his weaknesses, his stunts, his surprises. She'd listened to him, learned from him.

"Watch the jurors walk into the courtroom. Study their body language. See who's a leader and who's a follower. Eavesdrop on them. Pick their pockets. Steal their purses."

Figuratively speaking, he meant. Or did he?

Selecting a jury against Steve was like playing singles against Jackie Tuttle, her best bud. Jackie had a smooth, strong forehand and an okay backhand, but she was weak at the net. If Victoria hit to Jackie's backhand, then lured her to the net with a drop shot, she could blast passing shots for winners four times out of five.

Likewise, she knew Steve's game by heart.

"When you're picking a jury, don't forget that they're also picking you. They're deciding which lawyer they like better."

She'd learned so well, lately Steve had asked her to take the lead in questioning. For whatever reason, she made a better first impression. Okay, she *knew* the reason. She was gentle and kind, and it showed. Steve could be overly confrontational. Sure, he was graceful on his feet, but it was the grace of—*God help me*—a shark, cutting through the well of the courtroom, eager to bite off the head of a contrary witness, opposing counsel, or even the judge.

She knew something else about Steve's tactics, too. The weaker his case, the more outrageous his stunts. Meaning he would misbehave while questioning prospective jurors today. She didn't know how, but it was inevitable, like pesky mosquitoes following summer storms.

"Don't worry about jumping offsides. Sometimes the officials don't catch you."

Another of his lessons. At the first opportunity, he would start arguing his case. Voir dire—the questioning of jurors—is intended to detect prejudice or bias. Some trial lawyers wait until the opening statement to start planting seeds of their argument, which is still too soon, according to proper procedure. They do it because studies show that a sizeable percentage of jurors make up their minds in opening statements, *before* the first witness takes the stand.

But to Steve, opening statement was *too late.*

He starts arguing his case with "Good morning, Madame 'Persecutor.'"

Victoria would be on high alert. At least as prosecutor, she would start first. "Good morning, ladies and gentlemen," she began.

She carefully framed her questions to explain the highly technical charge of felony murder. "Do all of you understand that the defendant can be found guilty, even though someone else pulled the trigger?"

Numbers one through twelve nodded eagerly, a jury box of bobbleheads.

"It's never enough for the sheep to baa in unison.

Get in their faces, one-on-one, and challenge their be-liefs."

Steve again. Never trusting the voice of the crowd. He was right. You needed to separate the individuals from the pack, divide the leaders from the followers, the smart ones from the dummies.

"If you don't know who's gonna be foreman by the time the jury takes its oath, you haven't been paying attention."

Victoria spent the next hour going through her prepared questions and listening intently to each answer. Then she reviewed her chart. It was a twelve-grid document with sliding tabs where she could slip prospective jurors in and out of their slots. Number three had a quizzical look on his face. Nobuchi Fukui, CPA. College educated, married, three children. Owned his own home in Kendall, commuted downtown to his accounting firm. A decent prosecution juror.

"Mr. Fukui," she said. "A man doesn't pull the trigger, but he's charged with murder. Does that rule seem harsh to you?"

"Not at all. Not if the fellow precipitated the violence. People have to take responsibility for their actions. That's what's wrong with this country."

"Thank you, Mr. Fukui." Not just a decent prosecution juror. A *great* prosecution juror. She turned to the judge. "Your Honor, we tender the panel to Mr. Solomon."

Steve bounded to his feet and took up his position an even five feet from the rail of the jury box. No legal pad. No twelve-grid chart. He prided himself on being able to remember a dozen names and attach the right one to each juror.

"Let's start with you, sir. Mr. Fukui."

"Yes, sir," Fukui said suspiciously.

"Here's a real case. Two teenage boys, neither one armed, try to break into a warehouse out near the airport. They're not very good burglars, never did it before, and they can't even get inside. Now, here come the cops. They chase the boys across a field. A cop shoots and kills one of the boys. Under Ms. Lord's theory, the other boy must be convicted of felony murder. He'll spend the rest of his life in prison."

"Objection, Your Honor." When a puppy is naughty, Victoria knew, you have to quickly show who's the boss. "It's not my *theory*. It's the *law*."

"But is it justice?" Steve shot back.

"That's not the issue," Victoria retorted.

"Now, there's an admission for you," Steve proclaimed, turning to the jury with a knowing look. "The prosecutor believes in law without mercy. Law without justice. A cold, hard, *unfeeling* law."

"Your Honor!" Victoria pealed, trying to get Judge Gridley's attention.

"Okay, you two." The judge sighed. "We're gonna get through jury selection without any caterwauling. Now, Mr. Solomon, ask your questions and quit your speechifying."

"Of course, Your Honor." Steve turned back to Nobuchi Fukui. "Now, sir, let me take you back to that warehouse. In fact, let me take all twelve of you back there."

For a moment, two jurors seemed poised to get out of their seats, as if a bus was waiting to drive them to a warehouse near the airport.

"Mr. Fukui," Steve continued, "do you think the kid who bungled that burglary should be convicted of murder?"

"Well, it's not really up to me," the man said. "If that's what the law says..."

Perfect, Victoria thought. Make Nobuchi Fukui the foreman.

"The *law*," Steve said dismissively. "The law once said that women couldn't vote. The law once said that certain folks had to ride in the back of the bus. The law once said the government..." He stabbed a finger toward Victoria, as if she were the face of Evil. "...yes, the government, could lock up innocent American citizens because of their Japanese ancestry."

How cheesy, Victoria thought. Next, Steve will be asking Mr. Fukui if he'd like sushi for lunch.

"Just because it's written in books doesn't make it right."

"Objection, Your Honor." Victoria was on her feet again. "Mr. Solomon hasn't even waited for the trial to start before seeking jury nullification."

"Ms. Lord's right," the judge said. "Mr. Solomon, you shall refrain from implying that the jury may disregard the law. That's my job." The judge seemed to ponder that for a moment. "That is, I'll instruct the jury on the law."

"Thank you, Your Honor," Steve said with a slight bow. Another one of his sneaky tricks. Acting as if he'd just won a motion when he'd been slapped in the face.

"This case is about the cruel and inhuman treatment of animals," Steve told the panel.

No, it's not, Victoria thought.

"Now, thanks to your questionnaires, I already know who among you have pets at home, and I feel quite a kinship with you." He moved closer to number four, a middle-aged woman with enough coppery hair for an osprey to make a nest. Eyeglasses dangled from a beaded chain around her neck. "Mrs. Overton, I'll bet you love that orange tabby of yours. I know I love mine."

Oh, Jesus. Steve doesn't have a tabby. He's allergic to cats. He curses at cats, from the ones who knock over the garbage can to the ones who sing "Memory" and "Mr. Mistoffelees."

Mrs. Overton beamed at Steve, instantly suckered by his bull.

"Would you be shocked to know, Mrs. Overton, that cat innards are used by some unscrupulous companies in the manufacture of women's cosmetics?"

"Oh, my goodness," she murmured, bringing a hand to her mouth.

"And that neuroscience labs operate on monkeys without anesthesia, for research purposes?"

"Barbaric," the woman agreed.

"And that the testicles of little puppies are crushed into a powder that some men use to enhance their own potency?"

"The beasts," Mrs. Overton whimpered.

Victoria didn't know how much of that was true and doubted that Steve did, either. When he was on a roll, he roared like a fiery preacher in a revival tent, promising riches for allegiance to the Solomonic way, threatening hell for followers of the state.

"Now, Mrs. Overton, my client, young Gerald over there..."

He pointed at *young Gerald,* who smiled sheepishly at the jurors.

"...has witnessed firsthand the terror and abuse suffered by helpless animals at the hands of heartless and greedy humans. And young Gerald's sole intent the night of the incident was to protect two magnificent dolphins, those most gentle and intelligent of creatures."

Mrs. Overton nodded. As did they all. A dozen citizens, good and true, horrified by the rampant abuses against animals.

"And what was it that young Gerald saw that night? Words alone cannot convey the images that were burned into his impressionable mind."

Steve bent down and reached into his briefcase.

What could he be after? Surely there were no files in there.

A cat!

Steve pulled a plump orange tabby out of his old trial bag, waved it over his head, wrapped two hands around the cat's neck, and pulled. Hard. Then harder, veins throbbing in his own neck.

"Mr. Solomon!" The judge sounded alarmed.

Elwood Reed, the bailiff, stirred from his slumber and even tried to get to his feet.

Mrs. Overton's lips trembled.

Suddenly, the cat ripped in half, the head in Steve's right hand, its body in his left.

Someone in the gallery screamed. Mrs. Overton seemed close to fainting. Another juror gagged.

Stuffing fluttered out of the cat like wispy feathers. The animal was real, or had been. A prior owner had the little tabby stuffed. Steve must have picked it up at one of those dusty curio shops on Calle Ocho.

"Here's what shaped young Gerald Nash!" Steve thundered. "This is what molded him into a young man who would risk his own life to save the lives of sweet, defenseless animals!"

Victoria leapt to her feet. She was about to object when she noticed Steve's eyes calmly panning the jury box. Taking inventory. Checking facial expressions. Counting his votes. The horrified ones were defense jurors. The bemused ones, including Nobuchi Fukui, CPA, who wore a slight smile, were prosecution jurors.

"Your Honor," Victoria said calmly, "I wonder if decapitating a stuffed cat is proper use of voir dire."

"Certainly not before lunch." Judge Gridley hit the button and tooted his steam whistle. "Let's get some victuals and report back at one-thirty sharp."

* * *

Steve and Victoria shared an elevator on the way down to the cafeteria. He seemed to be waiting for her to say something. One of her bad-boy put-downs.

I won't give him the satisfaction.

After a moment, he said, "Well, I guess I woke everybody up."

Still she kept quiet, adding a yawn for emphasis. Or maybe de-emphasis.

"Okay," he said. "You're really mad at me, but you won't show it."

"My, you're so good at reading people, Mr. Solomon."

"Sarcasm doesn't become you, cupcake."

"I was going to do you a solid just now." She shook her head, sadly. "But that 'cupcake' thing..."

"Why's that upset you? I don't care if you call me 'studmuffin.'"

"I *don't* call you 'studmuffin.'"

"But if you want to, it's okay. Now, what's the solid you want to do me?"

The elevator door opened and they stepped into the

lobby. A swarm of hungry office workers headed toward the cafeteria.

"Wellfleet Dynamics, Inc.," she said.

"What?"

"The license plate you gave me. Those two guys who grabbed you."

"Yeah?"

"The Lincoln is registered to a Florida corporation called Wellfleet Dynamics, Inc. I'm not sure how it helps you, but there it is."

"Where are they located?"

"They're not. Corporation's inactive. It was formed by a lawyer in Tampa in 1989, the same day he formed Wellfleet Financing, Wellfleet Aerodynamics, Wellfleet Navigation, and a bunch of others. They're all shell corporations."

"Someone's gotta own their stock."

"Secretary of State's records don't show shareholders."

"The lawyer who filed the papers. What's his name?"

"Tully Meadows of St. Petersburg. Died in 1998."

They paused at the door to the cafeteria. Two leather-booted motorcycle cops strutted by, in the middle of a joke about pulling over Janet Jackson.

"Was she speeding?"

"Nah. She had one headlight out."

"How does an inactive corporation renew the car's registration every year?" Steve asked.

"I'd guess the parent company sends a check. But DMV—"

"Doesn't keep records of who pays the fee, just whether it gets paid."

"Right." There was some satisfaction in their ability to finish each other's sentences, she thought.

"I need to find the parent company," he said.

"Even if you do, how will it help you defend Gerald Nash?"

"One step at a time, Vic. A leads to B, and B leads to C. Those guys who snatched me hired Sanders. Which means Wellfleet, or whoever owns Wellfleet, needed someone who knew about dolphins. When I find out who that is, I'll know what they were gonna do with the dolphins. And maybe that will answer the question of why Grisby blasted the shit out of Sanders."

"Seems like too many questions, too many steps," she said.

"But if I get it right, Vic, the last step will prove that Gerald Nash is innocent."

Twenty-seven

EVEN STEPHEN

Victoria headed off for lunch with one of her witnesses, and Steve searched for his posse. He found Marvin (The Maven) Mendelsohn and Teresa Toraño, those septuagenarian lovebirds, coming out of the cafeteria.

Steve quickly asked Teresa to use her prodigious Internet skills—she'd signed up for AOL the first day of its existence—to help him figure out who owned Wellfleet Dynamics, Inc.

"Only if I tell Victoria everything I tell you," Teresa replied. "*Quedamos parejos.*"

"Even-Stephen, Stephen," Marvin added. "We gotta stay neutral."

"Jeez, Marvin. I'm at war here, and you're going Switzerland on me."

"If we were gonna choose sides, Stephen, it'd be the *shayna maidel*, not you."

"Marvin, what are you saying? You and I go way back."

"Nothing personal, boychik, but those animal rights guys are just thugs and terrorists."

"Forget my client," Steve implored him. "What about me?"

For years, Steve had bought corned beef sandwiches—*"with extra fat, if you don't mind, boychik"*—for Marvin and the Courthouse Gang. And now this. Steve considered The Maven a pal. More than that, a grandfather figure, and a terrific asset in trial. Marvin used forty years' experience selling women's shoes to help Steve in jury selection.

"Women with open-toed sandals are good for the defense. Conservative black pumps, good for the state."

Marvin had some theories about purses, too, but Steve couldn't tell a real Gucci from a knockoff, so that didn't do him much good.

"I can't believe you two are bailing on me," Steve complained.

"You're asking too much," Teresa said. "*A nosotros nos encanta* Victoria."

"Teresa's right," Marvin agreed. "It's not that we don't love you. We just love Victoria, too."

An hour later, having agreed to his posse's Even-Stephen terms, Steve huddled at the defense table with his client. Ten feet away, Victoria flipped through her color-coded note cards. The judge and jury had not yet returned from the lunch recess. Marvin and Teresa sat in the front row of the gallery, equidistant from the state and the defense tables. Marvin thumbed through a copy of *Ladies' Footwear Quarterly*. Even though he'd sold his shoe store many years earlier, he kept up with the trade. Teresa, her fingers still nimble, and perfectly manicured, worked on her laptop computer. She wrote a daily blog called "Abuela Cubana," where she'd been extolling the virtues of organic arthritis medicines and giving out the recipe for roasting a whole pig for Christmas Eve dinner.

Before she'd retired and turned over her businesses to her children, Teresa had owned a chain of funeral homes—Funeraria Toraño—a jai alai fronton, and a Chevrolet dealership. She was an astute businesswoman and often helped Steve in cases that required some knowledge of accounting.

Teresa was a handsome woman with charcoal hair, thanks to regular salon visits. She wore a strand of pearls with a stylish black silk dress. Marvin, bald since he was a corporal in the Korean War, wore plaid pants, a turquoise Banlon shirt, and a madras sport coat that had been very briefly in style in the 1970's. The two were madly in love.

Teresa glanced at Marvin, who waved to get their attention. "Stephen. Victoria. Come back here. Both of you."

Steve hustled through the swinging gate, then belatedly held it open for Victoria.

Teresa smiled up at both of them. Her laptop computer rested just where it belonged, in her lap. "This is very fast, mind you, so I don't have all the answers. But if you cross-reference Wellfleet Dynamics and all those other Wellfleets on file in Tallahassee with similar names incorporated in other states, you'll find they're all owned by a holding company called 'Cheyenne Range, Inc.,' a Delaware company."

"What's Cheyenne do?" Steve asked.

"Nothing. It's just a holding company. But it's owned by a Bermuda trust called 'Island Group Investments.' Whoever formed that company made it hard to trace back, but whoever owns Island owns Cheyenne and therefore owns all the Wellfleets."

"And the owner of all the Wellfleets is ... ?"

Teresa waved a finger at him. "A publicly traded corporation. A big one. Four billion in sales. Hardcastle Energy Services."

Teresa clicked a key on her laptop, and the Hardcastle website flicked onto the monitor. Rugged men in hard hats, oil platforms in the Gulf of Mexico, tankers at sea.

"The oil company?" Victoria said.

Steve was puzzled, too. Hardcastle owned chemical plants, refineries, and pipelines. The company was in the news when it helped put out the fires in Kuwait's oil wells after Desert Storm.

"Not just an oil company," Teresa told them. "They're a defense contractor, too. Submersibles, body armor, night vision goggles. Hundreds of items for the military."

"Fine," Steve said. "But why would Hardcastle send two guys to roust me? Why do they care what Gerald Nash knows?"

"*No sé.* But they also make communications equipment for the military."

"So does AT&T," Steve said. "So what?"

"*Ten paciencia,* Stephen. Have patience."

Teresa clicked the "Defense Subsidiaries" button on the screen. An instant later, a new picture appeared. Two dolphins arcing from the water, both with white harnesses circling their bodies. One harness was fixed with an antenna, the other with a camera.

"The communications gear is for dolphins," she said, hitting another button. The image changed. Six dolphins in a turquoise sea, all swimming fast enough to leave foamy wakes. Printed over the image were the words: "Keeping Ports Safe at Home and Abroad. The Marine Mammal Strike Force."

"Holy shit," Steve said. "There's a new villain in the courtroom. Hardcastle Energy Services. Big, rich, powerful. What more could I ask for?"

"A defense based on the evidence," Victoria suggested tartly.

"Sanders was an ex–Navy SEAL who handled dolphins. He worked for two guys from Hardcastle, a defense contractor that provides dolphins for the military. Like I said before, A leads to B, and B leads to C."

"Okay. Keep going. Where's C lead?"

"Jeez, give me a couple hours. By dinner tonight, I'll have my theory of the case, and I'll spell it out for you."

"I can hardly wait."

"Here's the crazy thing, Vic. My client's always railing about the military-industrial complex. An unholy alliance between big business and warmongering politicians. The State Attorney is just a tiny cog in a big wheel of conspiracies and corruption. All that left-wing boilerplate from a guy who's not very bright. But you know what, Vic? Gerald Nash is right. The bastard's been right from day one."

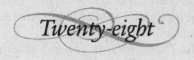

Twenty-eight

THE BASHERS

Coach Kreindler told Bobby he could pitch. But only in practice. And only to two batters.

Still, it was something. Whatever Uncle Steve had said to the coach—or whatever he'd threatened—had worked.

But where's Uncle Steve now?

A sticky evening. Mosquitoes and no-see-um gnats were buzzing in the glow of the field lights. Bobby was already lathered in sweat and his glasses were fogged.

On the mound, Bobby nervously toed the dirt the way he'd seen pitchers do on TV. One difference. Those guys never caught their spikes on the rubber and tripped. He'd nearly fallen twice and hadn't yet thrown a pitch.

Uncle Steve was late. He'd called from the car, saying traffic was backed up on Dixie Highway. Bobby had wanted to ask a question about his grip for the fastball, but his uncle was focused on his trial.

"Bobby, what do you know about the Marine Mammal Strike Force?"

"Not much. It's mostly classified."

"But you've heard of it."

"There's stuff on the Internet, but no way to know if it's true."

"What kind of stuff?"

"Dolphins being trained to fire toxic darts at enemy divers or drag them under and drown them, that kind of thing."

"Jesus. Gives new meaning to the term 'wet work.'"

"Suicide missions, too. Dolphins loaded with explosives to attack terrorists' boats. Really weird stuff."

"Is that real?"

"Dunno. You'd have to really be a sicko to do that to a dolphin."

Now Bobby wondered, just how could he pitch without his uncle here?

"Let's go, Robert," Coach Kreindler yelled from behind home plate. He was wearing a *"Kreindler Means Kosher"* T-shirt and leaning over the catcher in the umpire's position.

Barry Roth stood in the batter's box, crowding the plate. Thin, wiry, the Bobcats' leadoff hitter. Quick wrists, a singles hitter. Not a bad kid, at least compared to Rich (The Shit) Shactman.

The catcher was Miguel Juarez. His family didn't belong to Beth Am, but Miguel's dad was the security guard at the synagogue, and none of the Jewish kids wanted to catch. Miguel had short, thick legs, and could throw out a runner at second without ever coming out of his crouch. Bobby looked in for the sign. Miguel wiggled one finger.

Fastball.

Bobby worked the ball in his hand, his index and middle fingers running across the seams. He wound up, a jumble of herky-jerky motions. He looked unco-ordinated. But his arm was a whip.

He let fly.

The ball sailed straight toward Barry Roth's head.

Barry's legs flew out from under him as he hit the dirt, the ball rocketing all the way to the backstop.

"Ball one!" Coach Kreindler shouted. "Robert, watch it out there. No brushbacks."

But Uncle Steve had told him not to be afraid to throw inside.

"The inside of the plate is yours. You have to take it away from the batter."

A shudder ran through him. What if he hit Barry? What if he *hurt* him?

"What are you waiting for, Solomon? Chanukah?" Rich Shactman yelling from the on-deck circle. The jerk was swinging three bats, showing off his muscles.

Miguel Juarez signaled for another fastball. Bobby wound up and threw again. High and wide. Miguel came out of his crouch to nab it. Ball two.

Barry Roth crowded the plate even more. Another pitch, Bobby tensing up and hanging on too long. The ball skidded in the dirt before it reached the plate. Ball three.

Where are you, Uncle Steve?

Bobby tried to relax, but he couldn't. He tightened his grip even more, and the ball squirted out of his hand like a watermelon seed. A floater that looked like slow-pitch softball, going straight up and falling ten feet in front of the plate.

"Ball four!" Kreindler yelled. "One more batter, Robert."

The coach seemed pleased, as if letting Bobby pitch had been both annoying and a waste of time.

"Rich, get in there and take a couple swings," Kreindler said, smiling at his slugger.

Swaggering to the plate, Rich Shactman glared at Bobby, who took a shaky breath, picked up the resin bag, bounced it in his pitching hand a couple times, then tossed it away.

Stalling.

Tension gripped Bobby, a hundred pigeons flapping inside his chest. He tried to remember everything Uncle Steve taught him.

The grip. The windup. The release. I've forgotten everything.

"C'mon, Robert," Coach Kreindler yelled. "We only have the field for an hour."

"Which ends in two dang minutes," came another voice. A husky man in a pin-striped baseball jersey stood at the fence along the first-base line, his gut hanging over the steel railing. Shug Moss. Coach of the First Baptist Bashers.

A dozen kids in Bashers uniforms sidled up to the fence alongside Moss. Most seemed bigger than Rich Shactman. The ones who weren't had the long, lean look of sprinters or Dominican outfielders.

"Git a move on, Kreindler!" Shug Moss shouted. "You can't hog the field. It ain't kosher."

The Bashers laughed at their coach's southern-fried wit. Kreindler offered a feeble wave of his hand.

Moss had been a three-sport star athlete at Homestead High thirty years earlier. Having failed to show up for any classes his senior year, he forfeited a variety of college scholarship offers and signed a minor league baseball contract. A ferocious fastball hitter, his line drives splintered outfield fences in Dunedin, Lakeland, and other bush league towns. In four years, he got a shot with the Baltimore Orioles. He had one hit in thirty-four at-bats before being sent back to Double A ball. Just as he had failed basic grammar in high school, he never learned to hit a breaking pitch in the minors.

These days, when tanked on gin, he still talked about making it to The Show. His favorite story was to recall a blast into the upper deck at Yankee Stadium. Unfortunately, it was batting practice, and the ball was foul by fifty feet.

Now, Moss sold disability insurance, but his prime objective in life was to win the championship in the Kendall Sunday School Baseball League. He'd succeeded the last four seasons with a team composed not only of members of the First Baptist Church but also of undocumented Haitians who looked old enough to vote and a couple of players who had honed their skills in the Miami-Dade Youth Corrections Facility. Truth was, Moss would play an Al Qaeda suicide bomber if he could lay down a decent bunt.

On the mound, Bobby looked nervously toward the hulking Bashers, itching to get on the field for practice.

"*Gib zich a traisel*, Robert," Kreindler urged him. "Let's get this over with."

Bobby started his motion, feeling like his arms and legs belonged to someone else. He let the pitch go too soon, and the ball sailed over the backstop.

Whoops and hollers from the Bashers along the fence.

"Ball one," Kreindler announced.

Bobby tried again. This time, the pitch sailed ten feet behind Shactman.

"Ball two."

"This your new pitcher?" Shug Moss taunted. "Stevie Wonder has better control."

Bobby wiped the sweat off his glasses, then threw another fastball, this one skittering across the plate.

"Ball three," Kreindler called out.

Shug Moss smirked. His players laughed and high-fived.

Shactman stepped out of the batter's box. "This is embarrassing, Coach. The Bashers think we're all wee-nies."

He's embarrassed, Bobby thought, hating all those eyes on him.

"Robert, just relax," Coach Kreindler shouted. "Lay one right down the pipe."

Shactman stepped back into the batter's box.

Bobby took a smaller windup and floated a pitch chest high across the middle of the plate.

Shactman jumped on the pitch with a ferocious swing. A cannon shot, the crack of metal hitting leather. A rising rocket, the ball soared toward left field, gaining height and speed, never seeming to hit its apogee. The ball was still rising as it cleared the wooden fence and bounced high into a strand of live oak trees.

Holy shit!

Once at Pro Player Stadium, at a Giants-Marlins game, Bobby had seen Barry Bonds launch a home run that left the yard so fast, it seemed to be over the fence before Bonds had finished his swing. Outside of that, he had never seen a ball hit so hard.

Shactman still stood in the batter's box, like a golfer admiring a tee shot.

Kreindler rose up from his umpire's position and looked skyward. *"Got in himmel!"*

Shug Moss beamed toward Shactman. "Nice hitting, kid. Too bad you're on the wrong team." Then he turned to Bobby, who slumped toward the dugout. "And you! Four eyes. You ever think of taking up chess?"

Twenty-nine

NEVER TRUST THE SUITS

"I'm sorry I was late, kiddo," Steve said.

"Wouldn't have made any difference," Bobby sulked.

"Steve could have given you some tips," Victoria said.

"I'd still suck."

Victoria ran a hand through the boy's squashed hair, which bore the imprint of his ball cap. "Steve says you have potential. Something about your arm."

"A live arm." Steve made a throwing motion. "All you need is some confidence and a little practice."

Bobby picked up his root beer and sucked at the straw. He was deep into self-pity mode. They were sitting at an outdoor table at the Red Fish Grill in Matheson Hammock Park. The night was warm, but a breeze from the Bay cooled them. Across the water, they could see the lights of Key Biscayne. Some of those lights lined the dock at Cetacean Park, but from this distance, you couldn't really make out the place.

Bobby looked toward the darkness of the bay. "I don't wanna talk about baseball, okay?"

"How about the case, then?" Steve asked. "You really helped me today, kiddo."

"You're patronizing me, Uncle Steve."

"I mean it. You helped me prove that Hardcastle kidnapped Spunky and Misty."

"Prove it?" Victoria tried not to sound skeptical as she sipped at her Pinot Noir.

"Think about it," Steve said. "Hardcastle needed the world's smartest dolphins for its Marine Mammal program. That was the motive for the raid."

"I don't want to diss your case," she said, "but Hardcastle's a New York Stock Exchange company. A four-billion-dollar company. A company in the public eye."

"You ever hear of Enron? Never trust the suits, Vic."

"*You're* a suit."

"I *wear* a suit. There's a difference."

"Still not buying it," she said. "All you've got is a theory, not proof."

"Really? Bobby, how long does it take to train dolphins?"

"Four or five years to get to Spunky and Misty's level." Bobby dipped a piece of his broiled mahimahi into a spicy tartar sauce.

"Don't you see, Vic? Hardcastle wins a contract to provide trained dolphins to the military to guard the ports. But they don't have five years to do it. The clock's ticking. Fort Lauderdale. Long Beach. New York. Every port authority wants to be protected *yesterday*. They also want the sexiest, newest item in the defense arsenal, dolphins with cameras and transmitters, and for all we know, dart guns and iPods."

Victoria sipped at her wine, shook her head. "I still can't see a giant company taking a risk like that."

"Forget that Hardcastle's a billion-dollar conglomerate. It's made of divisions and departments. Somewhere there's a guy running the dolphin program, and he reports to a numbers cruncher who reports to a hard-ass who reports to the guy who runs all their defense subsidiaries. If the dolphin guy can't produce, there's no year-end bonus. There's bad publicity. If it's bad enough, *60 Minutes* comes knocking on your door. There are congressional investigations. Cries of boondoggles and pork-barrel politics. Taxpayer money down the drain. Hardcastle loses bigger contracts just because they couldn't supply dolphins who can do the job."

Victoria thought it over a moment. In the nearby saltwater pond, a pair of yellow-crowned herons poked their beaks in the shallows for crabs. "Let's say you're right and Hardcastle doesn't have time to train its own dolphins. Why not just *buy* them?"

"Mr. Grisby loves Spunky and Misty," Bobby said. "He'd never sell them."

"Even if Grisby wanted to, he couldn't do it," Steve said. "Think of the uproar. One day, Spunky and Misty are nuzzling kids with muscular dystrophy. The next day, they're packing explosives. I don't think so."

A waiter came to their table with offers of key lime pie and *tres leches* cake. Bobby went for the pie. Victoria ordered cinnamon apple tea, and Steve stood pat.

"If Hardcastle's as corrupt as you say, what's a retired naval officer like Sanders doing mixed up with them?" Victoria asked.

"I figure he was a legitimate hire, the perfect guy to run the dolphin-training program. Then Hardcastle tells Sanders he has twelve months to produce, and he says it can't be done. They say make it happen. Again, he says it's impossible. Finally, they put someone else in charge, two guys from their security division, or whatever they call their department of dirty pool."

"The men in the Lincoln," Victoria said.

"They tell Sanders they've got a shortcut. Steal trained dolphins. But they need cover. It's got to look like the Animal Liberation Movement is behind it."

"So Sanders dupes Nash? That's your theory?"

"A perfect plan. Sanders and his buddies can hit several attractions around the country and blame the animal nuts. This was the first raid, and it blew up in their faces."

Victoria sipped her tea.

Steve waited.

In the saltwater pool, a long-necked white ibis with a curved beak joined the herons in their search for dinner.

Victoria sipped some more, then said, "I think you may be right."

"Yes! I knew it. I knew you'd respond to logic and reason. You always do."

"Your client was clueless, wasn't he?"

"Yep. Nash figured they were setting the dolphins free. He'd have shit a brick if he knew they were turning the animals into warriors."

"Not that it would matter if Nash knew." Victoria put down the teacup and patted her lips dry. "It's irrelevant that his accomplices were committing a different crime. Regardless of their motive or his, Nash committed a *felony,* Steve. Grand larceny. In the course of that felony, Sanders was killed. So even if you prove to the jury everything you just said, you still have no defense. Your client is still guilty."

SOLOMON'S LAWS

9. Be confident, but not cocky. Smile, but don't snicker. And no matter how desperate your case, never let the jurors see your fear.

Thirty

SPEECHLESS

Steve sat at the defense table, slumped and frowning, in blatant disregard of his rules of courtroom behavior. He'd taught Victoria that a trial lawyer should always project confidence.

"It's your courtroom. Not the judge's. Not the jury's. Not the snoring bailiff's. Let everybody know you're in charge."

Victoria delivered her opening statement with competence and ease. Clearly she'd learned her lessons.

Steve had a blank yellow pad on the table in front of him, his client Gerald Nash beside him. Victoria was doing just what Steve expected. No frills, no riffs, no fancy footwork. Just solid, likeable lawyering. She started by reading the indictment. Prosecutors often do that. The formal language tends to convey to the jury that Zeus himself had leveled the charges.

"The Grand Jurors of the State of Florida, duly called, impaneled and sworn to inquire and true presentment make . . ."

Steve briefly considered an old trick.

"It's just a piece of paper, folks."

Then he would tear the indictment in half. But Victoria would be ready for the stunt. She'd seen him do it before.

"I'm going to give you a preview of the evidence," Victoria told the jury. "But before I do, there's one image I want you to see."

She picked up a poster board and positioned it in front of the jury. A head shot of Sanders in his dress whites. Handsome. Rugged. Still alive.

Nice move, Vic.

He'd always told her to humanize her clients. Now, while the State of Florida was technically her client, she wanted the jurors to connect with the late Chuck Sanders.

"This is Lieutenant Commander Charles Sanders," Victoria said. "He grew up in a small town in South Carolina and worked summers as a lifeguard. He earned a swimming scholarship to Vanderbilt and enrolled in the Reserve Officers Training Corps because he wanted to serve his country. In the U.S. Navy, he survived the most rigorous training known to the military, and he became a Navy SEAL. A decorated war hero in Desert Storm, he . . ."

Steve tuned her out and watched the jurors. All twelve were transfixed. Victoria was a natural. Poise and presence. You didn't have to hear her words. Just look at her in her double-breasted jacket and matching skirt that fell just below the knees. Brown pinstripes, wide lapels. Gucci or Prada or Fendi. One of the Italian designers; he couldn't tell them apart. Victoria looked great whatever she wore. Smart and stylish and sexy.

At that moment, Steve was aware of two conflicting feelings. Despair at the knowledge that he would lose the case, and a reservoir of warmth, an ocean of love, for the woman who was going to defeat him.

"Now Charles Sanders is dead," Victoria continued. "Killed as a direct result of a crime committed by the defendant, Gerald Nash."

She pointed toward the defense table, her pinstriped arm steady, her lacquered nails glistening.

The jury turned toward Nash, who winced and squirmed in his chair. In his ill-fitting suit with its lumpily knotted tie, he couldn't look more guilty if he'd been foaming at the mouth and howling at the moon.

Victoria smoothly moved on to a discussion of the elements of the crime, describing exactly how Nash's actions fit every one.

Steve drifted off again. Victoria had been right the day before when she said he had no defense. Sure, he may have solved a mystery. He knew what Sanders was doing and who he worked for, but so what? Steve had spent so much time tracking down loose ends, he hadn't done the scut work of defending his client. Now he needed to do something he'd never done before in a criminal trial. When the judge turned to him, Steve would politely decline to give his opening statement. He would wait until after the state rested its case, then belatedly concoct something to say.

This strategy—or lack of strategy—violated yet another one of his rules, based on the psychological concept of "primacy." People are more receptive to information at the *beginning* of an event than in the middle or at the end. Sure, some lawyers believe in "recency," that people remember best what they hear *last*. But Steve always told Victoria to get off to a quick start.

"A flurry of punches, knock 'em out in the first round."

But here he was, reserving opening statement until after he heard the state's evidence, because he had no winning strategy.

Speechless.

He scanned the gallery. Marvin the Mavin and Teresa Toraño sat in the front row, holding hands. They nodded with approval as Victoria crisply explained the difference between peaceful protests protected by the First Amendment and trespasses and larceny, which are crimes.

"She's good," Nash whispered, sounding alarmed.

Of course she is, Steve thought, I taught her everything. No, that wasn't true. A person isn't a dolphin. You don't blow a whistle and hold up a mackerel to teach a person how to try a case. They either have the innate talent or they don't.

Some people can throw a baseball a hundred miles an hour and knick a slice of airspace sixty feet, six inches away.

Some people can recite eighty-verse limericks from memory without blowing a line.

And some people can tell a story that will move a dozen strangers to either condemn or exonerate another human being.

While Steve mulled over these thoughts, Victoria began wrapping up, warmly thanking these good folks for leaving their jobs and families to come downtown and help do justice. The good folks beamed back at her, mighty proud to be of service.

The courtroom door opened and a woman took a seat in the last row. Mid-twenties, maybe. Difficult to tell her age because she wore wraparound sunglasses and a little white tennis jacket with a high collar turned up. Maybe it was the sunglasses. Maybe it was the style of her upswept blond hair. Or maybe it was the courtroom setting. Whatever the reason, Steve thought of Lee Remick in the classic movie *Anatomy of a Murder*. A woman of mystery and dubious credibility.

His client followed his gaze and seemed to squint. "Huh," Nash said.

"Huh, what?"

"For a second, that woman looked like passion."

It took Steve a second to realize Nash meant "Passion" with a capital "P." Passion Conner. His girlfriend and accomplice, who'd hung him out to dry.

"But it's not her," Nash said.

Steve tried to get a better look at the newcomer. "You sure?"

"Yeah. Passion's not a blonde."

"You ever hear of beauty salons?"

Steve stood and took a step toward the gate that led to the gallery. The woman looked up at him, her body stiffening.

Steve moved through the gate and headed for her.

"Mr. Solomon!" Judge Gridley called out.

Steve ignored him. The woman bounded to her feet. She moved toward the door.

The judge hit his steam whistle. Spectators jerked up in their seats.

The woman pushed through the door to the corridor.

"Mr. Solomon! Ms. Lord hasn't finished her opening. You don't jump off a moving train—"

"Sorry, Judge. But nature calls."

"Now?"

"Those cafeteria burritos, Your Honor."

He was out the door before the judge could reply.

* * *

In the corridor, Steve wheeled left, then right. Caught a glimpse as the woman turned a corner at the escalators. Six flights down to the lobby. He could beat her there by taking the stairwell.

He ran to the stairwell door, nearly knocking over two young lawyers in spiffy suits, sniffing the halls of Justice for fresh business. Steve took the steps two at a time, vaulting over the bannister to cut corners at each landing.

The floors flew by.

He burst through the door into the lobby.

The usual suspects. Cops. Corrections officers. Clerks. Public defenders, prosecutors. Spectators and witnesses and downtown lawyers. Milling about, buzzing like bees in a hive.

Steve waited at the bottom of the escalator. No blonde in a tennis jacket, with or without sunglasses. Maybe she got off the escalator on one of the higher floors, then switched to the elevator. Steve hurried to the elevator bank. A dozen people poured out of two cars. She wasn't among them.

Damn.

No use standing here. He had to do something. And he had to get back to the courtroom before Judge Gridley held him in contempt.

Steve took the down escalator up, catching stares from the security guards and glares from the people he passed, going the wrong way. From lobby to second floor, then second floor to third.

And there it was.

A blond wig sticking out of a trash can. A white tennis jacket jammed underneath.

"Mr. Solomon."

A man's sleepy voice.

Elwood Reed, in his baggy bailiff's uniform. Reaching into his pocket.

Oh, shit. Am I gonna be handcuffed?

"Judge thought you might need these," Reed said, handing Steve a small bottle of pills.

Steve peered at the label. "Equilactin?"

"Judge says it'll help form solid stools."

"Well, he oughta know," Steve allowed.

Thirty-one

CLUELESS

"You're sure the woman was Nash's ex-girlfriend?" Victoria asked.

"Why else would she run from me like that?" Steve answered.

"She could be *your* ex-girlfriend."

"She never calls Nash, then shows up at the trial. Now, why would she do that?"

"What does Nash say?"

"No idea. He's still heartbroken she ran out on him in the first place."

They were sitting in the backyard of their home on Kumquat Avenue, Victoria sipping Chardonnay, Steve knocking back a Morimoto Ale. Friday night. On Monday morning, Victoria would put Wade Grisby on the witness stand, and Steve had nothing to poke holes in his story. A bleak thought occurred to him.

Maybe Grisby's telling the truth. Maybe he was only defending himself when he gunned down Sanders.

There was nothing to tie Grisby to Hardcastle. There was no evidence Grisby had ever encountered Sanders before the raid. Without some link, without some motive for Grisby to kill Sanders, Steve had nothing.

Zilch. Bupkes. Gornisht.
Guilty as charged.
"I've never felt so clueless in a trial," he said.
"Are you gaming me?"
He shook his head. "You're going to beat me. But that's not what's bothering me. I'm letting Nash down. He's just a naive kid who deserves better."

* * *

She heard it in his voice. He was wounded.
"You've got lots of clues," she said. "You just don't know where they lead."
"Are you trying to tell me something?"
She didn't answer, just took another sip of the wine.
"Because if you know something about Passion Conner," he pressed her, "under the discovery rules, you better tell me."
"You don't have to remind me about my ethical duties. And I don't know anything about Passion Conner, except I'm glad my parents weren't as creative when it came time for the baby naming."
"She could be connected to Sanders," Steve said. "They both sought out Gerald Nash. When Sanders suggested they hit Cetacean Park, Passion cheered him on. When Nash tried to call her, she'd already canceled her cell phone. The backstory she gave him, Marine Biology degree from Rosenstiel, was phony. No one with that name ever attended the school. And crewing on a tuna boat, getting radicalized in the animal rights movement. No way to disprove it, but I doubt it's true."
Victoria tried nudging him in another direction. "If you're at a dead end with her, why not focus on Sanders?"

"I already know who he was—an ex–Navy SEAL who went to work for Hardcastle."

"With a stop in between at an insurance company."

Steve laughed. "Yeah. His cover story. Nash told me."

Victoria gave him one of her looks. The one that came with a little shake of the head.

"What?" he asked.

"Did you go through the personal effects from Sanders' car?"

"Everything on your discovery list. A pre-paid calling card. Some shorts and Hawaiian shirts. A wallet with a bunch of hundred-dollar bills. No credit cards, no receipts from the laundry, no lottery tickets."

"So you didn't notice the business card. *'Charles J. Sanders. Chief Adjuster.'*"

"I saw it. Some phony insurance company."

"You're sure it's phony?"

"I could print a card saying I'm king of the world."

Victoria finished her wine and sighed. "You're getting sloppy, and you know why? Because I always do the detail work for you."

"What are you talking about?"

"Did you call the number on the card?"

"Of course. I got Sanders' voice mail. It was *his* cell phone, not an insurance company."

"Did you listen to his message?"

"It said he was unavailable. Which was a real understatement."

"And that's where you stopped?"

"Yeah. The technical legal term, Vic, is 'dead end.'"

"But you have his phone number. You could subpoena the carrier and find out the name on the account."

"Who would do that? No lawyer I know would do that." He paused a moment. "*You* did that?"

"I don't have to tell you anything else. I've given you more than the law requires. There's nothing that says I have to lead you by the hand."

"Nothing except your sense of justice. If I missed something that might result in an injustice, you'd tell me. And not just because we love each other. You'd do it no matter who was defending the case."

"Don't play me, Steve."

"Okay. Okay. I'll get a subpoena issued for the phone carrier. I'll get a process server. I'll be a real grind."

"Good."

"And when I get the records, what am I going to learn?"

"Steve!"

"You're right. You've helped enough. Thanks."

She sighed, a single breath of exasperation. "The cell phone is registered to an insurance company. Bestia Casualty. They're headquartered in Denver."

"They're real?"

"Sanders worked there. Chief Adjuster."

"I'm having trouble picturing Chuck Sanders in a white shirt and tie and holding a clipboard."

"It's not auto insurance. He wasn't appraising fender benders."

Steve seemed to think it over a moment. In the backyard bottlebrush tree, a mockingbird was calling to its mate. "Just what kind of insurance does Bestia sell?"

"Specialized business casualty."

"Specialized? What's that mean?"

Victoria poured herself more wine. "In the industry, it's what they call 'unusual risks.' "

"Unusual? What the hell's that mean?"

Her silence forced him to think about it. It took a moment. "Animal attractions?"

"Lots of them. Lion Safari. Monkey Palace. Sea-quarius."

"And Cetacean Park? And Grisby's other place. In California, the first one ALM raided."

"Undersea World," Victoria helped out.

"Bestia insured them, too?"

"I'm putting Grisby on the stand Monday morning. Why don't you ask him?"

"You're something else, Vic."

"I just want to level the playing field."

"You restore my faith in the justice system."

"Stop it. You'd do the same for me."

He didn't answer.

"Wouldn't you, Steve?"

* * *

An hour later, Steve knocked at the study door and waited.

"Come in," Victoria said.

The room was dark except for a lamp on an end table. Victoria was propped on two pillows on the convertible sofa, reading. She wore an orange silk camisole over white silk slacks, and somehow reminded Steve of a Creamsicle.

He moved toward the sofa bed, and she raised one hand. "Hold it right there, cowboy. You know the rules."

"I just want to talk, that's all."

"Uh-huh."

Steve sat on the corner of the sofa bed. "I think you just tanked your own case."

"How do you figure?"

"When I took Grisby's depo, he denied ever knowing Sanders. On cross, I'll prove he lied. His credibility will be shot, and no one will believe his version of the shooting."

"Grisby says he didn't know Sanders worked for the insurance company, and I believe him."

"How's that possible? Grisby would have filed a claim after Undersea World was hit."

"A junior adjuster handled everything on-site. All Sanders did was approve the paperwork back at the home office. Bestia's records confirm it."

"So you're saying this is just a big coincidence. The guy who approved the insurance payment after the first raid accidentally turns out to be the thief the second time."

"No coincidence at all. Sanders knew the location of every single trained dolphin in the country. Once Hardcastle hired him, he knew exactly where he could steal the best."

"I'm not buying it. I don't care what the paperwork shows. Grisby had to know Sanders and he had to want him dead."

"Why?"

"Because it's the only way my client goes free."

SOLOMON'S LAWS

10. Never sleep with a medical examiner, unless you're dead.

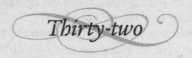

Thirty-two

SATURDAYS AT THE MORGUE

Steve flicked his wrist and jiggled the frying pan a foot above the burner. He prided himself on his ability to make a perfectly symmetrical apple-cheddar omelette, the cheese melting right to the edge without slopping over.

"Smells good," Victoria said, checking out the kitchen table. Toasted English muffins, freshly brewed coffee, and sliced papayas. "Someone wants something."

"Don't be so cynical, Vic. You know I like to make you breakfast on Saturday mornings."

"Only when you've been bad Friday night."

Bobby walked in, barefoot and wearing a Miami Heat jersey that hung to his knees. "Yum. Is it makeup time, Uncle Steve?"

"Hey, cut it out, you two." Steve served Victoria her omelette and started up another one. "Can't a guy do something nice for the people he loves?"

"Most people can. Bobby, why do you think your uncle's being so thoughtful?"

"No idea, but I'm cool with it." The boy speared a slice of papaya. "Can I pitch to you today, Uncle Steve?"

"As soon as we get back from the morgue."

"Great. Can I watch an autopsy?"

"Nope. We're just gonna meet with Dr. Ling."

"So, that's it," Victoria said. "You're witness-tampering today."

"Hey, I'm entitled to talk to your witnesses."

"You don't want me to tell Dr. Ling to stonewall you, is that it?"

"Dr. Ling won't talk to Uncle Steve, anyway," Bobby said. "Dr. Ling hates him."

Steve flipped the second omelette, his motion herky-jerky, the cheese slopping onto the pan. "No she doesn't, kiddo."

"I heard her say she'd like to cut your heart out."

"She's a medical examiner. It was a professional statement."

Not long before Steve met Victoria, he'd had a brief relationship with Dr. Mai Ling. He'd known her for several years from court, but they'd only got together after a marathon night of Texas Hold 'Em with a rowdy group of homicide detectives, ER doctors, and deputy medical examiners. Steve admired Mai's ability to keep her poker face whether bluffing, folding, or removing bullet fragments from a spleen. She was committed to her work, and would often cancel dinner dates after a drive-by shooting in Liberty City.

Mai was blatantly pro-prosecution. She was constantly irritated by Steve's courtroom antics on behalf of defendants. The tipping point came when he cross-examined her in a murder case, pointing out that she'd performed the autopsy the morning after consuming two bottles of Sauvignon Blanc and spending the night in a bed not her own. Steve didn't need a private investigator to ferret out the information, as he had provided both the wine and the bed. On her way out of the courtroom, Mai announced that she would, indeed, be pleased to perform an autopsy on Steve while he was still breathing.

"I could always tell when Dr. Ling slept over," Bobby said. "The house smelled like formaldehyde."

"She called it *'le parfum de la mort,'*" Steve said, "but to her, it smelled like roses."

"Uncle Steve, you sure dated a lot of weirdos, B.V."

Meaning "Before Victoria," Steve knew.

Victoria poured herself a cup of coffee. "You don't expect Dr. Ling to contradict her autopsy report, do you, Steve?"

"I just need her to refine a point or two."

"If she's holding a scalpel," Bobby said, "I know what she'd like to refine."

* * *

The county morgue was a red brick building that resembled a schoolhouse. It was located, not so humorously, on Bob Hope Road. Usually, Dr. Mai Ling spent Saturday mornings doing the paperwork that had piled up along with the bodies. But today she was perched on a stool in a spotless lab, gently brushing specks of tissue off a skull under a magnifying lens.

"Hey, Mai," Steve called out.

She turned and stared at him with the same poker face she used when pushing all-in on the river. Mai was a petite woman with short dark hair and a face with sharp planes and small features. She wore eye shadow the color of an eggplant. This, with her dark eyes, tended to give her a raccoon look. Her white lab coat was crisply starched.

"How's my favorite canoe maker?" Steve tried again. No smile. No nothing.

"Bobby," he continued, "did I ever tell you that Dr. Ling never had a patient who lived?"

Bobby rolled his eyes.

Still ignoring Steve, Mai smiled at the boy and held up the skull. "Bobby, do you know what I'm doing right now?"

"The skull has two different spiderweb fractures. You want to see which one caused the death because—and just guessing here—two different guys hit the dead guy."

"You're a very smart boy." Mai set the skull on the counter and turned toward Steve. "What brings you here on a Saturday, Counselor?"

"Same as you. Pursuing justice."

"If it's the Nash case, my autopsy report speaks for itself. I have nothing to add."

"I'm going to cross-examine you next week. Don't you want a preview?"

"Sure. Preferably without wine."

Steve spent a few minutes explaining what he wanted. Illustrations on the autopsy report showed the location of Sanders' wounds. Pellets from the first shotgun blast peppered the gluteus medius muscle of the hip and lodged in the iliac crest. But the femoral artery wasn't severed. Steve's question was simple and direct.

"Would that first shot have killed Sanders?"

"I know what you're getting at," Mai replied. "You want me to say the first shot disabled Sanders but wouldn't have killed him. Then you'll argue to the jury that Grisby's responsible for Sanders' death by firing the second shot needlessly."

"I want the truth, Mai. Nothing more, nothing less."

"Ha."

"C'mon. You're supposed to be impartial. You're a public employee, and my client's a member of that public."

"You want impartial? Here it is. I can't tell to a reasonable medical probability whether the first hit was a kill shot."

"I don't believe that. You're helping the home team, Mai, just like always."

"And just like always, you're being a total shit."

"Please. No profanity in front of the child," Steve said, with a straight face.

Bobby tossed off a laugh. "That's whacked, Uncle Steve."

"Mai, I'm gonna move to strike your testimony on account of bias and prejudice."

Mai's eyes blazed from beneath her purple eye shadow. "Dammit. I'm telling you the same thing I told the FBI agent. There's no way to know for certain whether—"

"What FBI agent? This is a state case."

"Great. Go tell it to Washington."

"C'mon, Mai. Who came to see you?"

"A female agent. I don't remember her name."

"I need to know who's mucking around in my case."

"Oh, you have needs? Well, guess what, Steve? So do I."

"Jeez, don't make this personal. Now, I know you, Mai. Anytime you talk to someone, you make a note in the file. Those files are public records. If I have to get a court order, I will."

"Bobby," Mai said. "Will you promise me that when you grow up, you won't be a defense lawyer?"

"I'm going to be a major league pitcher," the boy promised.

* * *

Six minutes later, Dr. Mai Ling reached into a file cabinet and handed Steve the file. It didn't take long for him to find what he wanted. Stapled inside the cover was a business card.

Constance Parsons. Special Agent. Federal Bureau of Investigation.

"Happy now?" Mai asked.

"Did she tell you why the FBI was involved in a state murder case?"

"She told me she was investigating. That's all."

"Constance Parsons," Steve said, as if the name might conjure up something. "What else can you tell me about her?"

"She's one of the young ones. You know how they are. Gung ho, until they get transferred to Missoula or Rapid City."

"Connie Parsons," Bobby said.

Steve gave him a look. "Constance. Connie. What difference does it make, kiddo?"

"Nothing much. Except her friends probably call her Connie."

"Yeah, probably. So?"

" 'Connie Parsons' is an anagram for 'Passion Conner,' " Bobby said.

Thirty-three

PITCHING PRACTICE

"Does this mean I can't pitch to you today?" Bobby asked.

"No way. We're gonna work on the circle change-up," Steve told him. "You've got to follow through all the way, make 'em think a fastball's coming."

They were in Steve's Mustang, headed down South Dixie Highway toward Coconut Grove.

"What about finding the FBI agent?" Bobby asked.

"A fastball's all about power. A change-up is about deception. I like the change-up."

"Uncle Steve. What about Connie Parsons?"

"Gonna take care of that right now."

Steve picked up his cell phone. It took a while to work through the automated menu of the local FBI office, but finally he reached a real person, the weekend operator.

"Agent Constance Parsons, please," Steve said.

"The office is closed today, sir."

"Do kidnappers and bank robbers know that?"

"Would you like to leave a message, sir?"

"My name's Steve Solomon. I know you have emergency contact numbers for all the agents. So please contact Agent Parsons immediately. Tell her to meet me for drinks at six o'clock at the Rusty Pelican on the causeway. I'm buying."

"Are you asking Agent Parsons out on a date, sir?"

"More or less. Please also tell her if she doesn't show, I'll subpoena her to testify in open court in the Nash case, and she'll never work undercover in this town again."

"Is there anything else, sir?"

"Only that I have her wig and sunglasses."

Steve clicked the phone off and winked at Bobby.

"Can I come along, Uncle Steve?"

"Nope. After we work out, I want you off your feet. You have a game tomorrow."

"It doesn't take much energy to stand in right field."

"You're pitching tomorrow, kiddo."

"Does Coach Kreindler know that?"

"Not yet. But I'll talk to him."

"Riii-ght."

"You gotta trust me, Bobby. On everything. At six o'clock today, I'm gonna solve the Nash case. And to-morrow, when the First Baptist Bashers come to the plate, you'll be pitching."

Thirty-four

THE PROVOCATEUR

The sun dipped toward the Everglades and painted a ribbon of clouds the color of pomegranates. The still water of Biscayne Bay sparkled with diamonds. It would have been a beautiful evening, Steve thought, if he didn't have to threaten an FBI agent over cocktails.

The Rusty Pelican sat on the north side of the Rickenbacker Causeway, halfway between the main-land and the island of Key Biscayne. Arriving early, Steve had parked his Mustang in the restaurant lot, walked across a tropical walkway over a man-made waterfall, and entered the place, a tourist trap with av-erage food but a stunning view of Miami's skyline across the Bay. The Pelican had burned down once, and been blown away a couple of times by hurricanes. But like a chopped-down melaleuca tree, it kept com-ing back to life.

Steve chose the meeting spot both for the view and the fact that Agent Parsons would be unlikely to shoot him in such a public place. Now he sat under a wicker paddle fan, nursing a Clase Azul tequila, watching a triangular sailboat race just outside the floor-to-ceiling windows.

He wondered if she would show up.

Passion Conner.

Animal rights activist. Girlfriend of the terminally dim Gerald Nash.

Constance Parsons.

FBI agent. Undercover operative. Instigator. And...

What's the word I'm looking for?

Provocateur.

Steve was on his second tequila when someone came up behind him. "Mr. Solomon."

Tall, great posture, athletic build. Brunette with a cute, Dorothy Hamill haircut. A blue canvas skirt with white stripes and a white cotton top with blue stripes. A sailor look. The handbag was made of straw and big enough to carry a gun, but not so big as to slow her down in a chase. She eased into the seat across from him at the small table.

"I don't know what to call you," Steve said. "Passion. Constance. Connie?"

"Agent Parsons will do."

"I didn't get a good look at you on the Jet Ski that night. But it was you, Agent Parsons."

"I was on duty. You know that now."

"You'd infiltrated the Animal Liberation Movement, but you didn't know what you'd gotten into."

"Not at first. But once Sanders came into the picture, we did a workup on him. We found the connection to Hardcastle, and the investigation expanded."

"Fraud in government contracts by a huge defense contractor. It's the parallel investigation the U.S. Attorney warned Pincher about."

"What about it?"

"Big, important case like that. You sure it's not a little over your pay grade?"

"Did you invite me here to insult me, Mr. Solomon?"

A waiter in a Hawaiian shirt stopped at their table, and Agent Parsons ordered a passion fruit iced tea. Passion Conner. Passion fruit. Sure, why not?

Steve waited until the waiter was out of earshot. "All I'm saying is that one day you're looking into some potheads knocking over puppy farms, and the next day you're taking on a four-billion-dollar company with political connections. And not doing it very well, I might add."

"What is it you want, Mr. Solomon?"

"I'm just wondering who's gonna take the fall for your screwup. You or your superior? And what's Hector Diaz say about all this? The U.S. Attorney can't be pleased when the FBI instigates a murder instead of investigating one."

"If you're talking about Sanders—"

"You encouraged Nash to go on that raid. He wanted to hit some pet stores in the malls. But you said, 'Let's go big-time. Let's do an amphibious assault on Cetacean Park.'"

"It was Sanders' idea, not mine."

"What's the difference? You went along with it."

"I was working undercover. Under Justice Department guidelines, when the proposed crime is nonviolent—"

"The 'proposed' crime," Steve interrupted, "turned into something else, didn't it?"

"There was no way of knowing that. I followed procedures."

"You *knew* who Sanders was. You knew he was armed, and you brought my nitwit client along. There you are, a federal agent, and you provoked a crime. You're the provocateur of a murder."

She was quiet a moment, pretending to watch a golden lionfish dart in and out of coral rock caves in a table-side aquarium.

"I'm going to ask you one last time, Mr. Solomon. Then I'm going to leave. What is it you want?"

The waiter delivered the iced tea with a straw and a flower sticking out of the glass.

"It's simple," Steve said. "Start a daisy chain over there in government land. Tell your boss to tell the U.S. Attorney to tell Pincher to tell Victoria to offer Nash a plea. Simple trespassing. Time served. Case over."

"It's not going to happen."

"Fine. I'll subpoena you. You can explain to the jury why my naif of a client should go to prison because the FBI encouraged him to take part in a crime that turned into murder."

"That sort of publicity would endanger the ongoing investigation of Hardcastle."

"To say nothing of your career, Agent Parsons."

Outside the windows, a trimaran with six partyers aboard slid quietly by, waving to the patrons inside.

"There may be one way I can help you," she said after a moment.

Steve waited, wishing he were on a sailboat instead of here, playing hardball with the Forces of Evil, aka the federal government.

"There were two men on a boat that night, waiting to pick up the dolphins. They work security for Hardcastle."

"We've met. They drive a Lincoln and offer rides to strangers."

"Is your client willing to testify against them?"

"Why do you need my client? You can ID them."

"Not without blowing my cover. We want to flip the two guys, go after Hardcastle executives for contract fraud and racketeering. If Nash will cooperate..."

"Consider it done. Where are the guys?"

"We don't know, but we'll find them."

"Ah, geez. I'm in the middle of trial. Once Nash gets convicted, it's too late."

"We're on their trail."

"Yeah. Them and Osama bin Laden."

"Look, Solomon, I'll do what I can to help Nash, but I can't make the case go away."

"What *can* you do?"

"Share intel."

"I'm listening."

"We had Grisby under surveillance. Sanders stopped by Cetacean Park two days before the raid."

"Did he talk to Grisby?"

"For about two or three minutes. Out on the dock. But we don't know what was said."

"It's not much, but it's something," Steve said. "Grisby claimed he never saw Sanders before the night he killed him."

"Another thing that never added up," Agent Parsons said. "On three consecutive nights before the raid, Grisby took the two dolphins into the Bay."

"What do you mean, 'took them'?"

"Around midnight, Grisby rode out to the channel on a Jet Ski and led the dolphins over to Hurricane Harbor. He left them there overnight, then went back in the morning and led them up the channel and into the park. Same thing each time."

"Why? Why would he do that?"

"No idea." Agent Parsons sipped the rest of her

passion fruit iced tea through the straw until it made an unladylike slurping sound. "It didn't seem relevant to our investigation of Hardcastle."

"Maybe not," Steve said. "But it might be damn relevant to why Grisby killed Sanders."

Thirty-five

DOLPHIN DOUBLES

"Training them," Bobby said.

"What do you mean?" Steve asked.

"Mr. Grisby must have wanted Spunky and Misty to know that if they ever left the channel, he'd come get them. He'd lead them back to the park."

"Is that even possible—training the dolphins to wait for him?"

"When you tell me to wait somewhere, what do I do?"

"Whatever you want."

"Spunky and Misty aren't like that. They try to please. And they want to be fed."

Steve was driving along Miracle Mile in Coral Gables and speaking into his cell phone. Bobby was at the house, watching an instructional baseball video with the sound turned down. He should have been taking a shower and getting ready for dinner. A Saturday night tradition. Steve always took Bobby and Victoria to whatever restaurant they chose to celebrate the weekend. Tonight, it was Restaurant St. Michel in the Gables.

"Grisby knew Sanders was coming for the dolphins,"

Steve said. "That's why he fired the security guard. That's why he had the shotgun. He prepared everything, including a safe place for the dolphins to hide until the shooting stopped."

"Makes sense, Uncle Steve. He'd lost his two best dolphins before and sure didn't want it to happen again."

Steve hit the brakes and pulled over to the curb. "Say that again."

"Say what? Mr. Grisby lost two dolphins before, and—"

"That's it, Bobby. It happened before! Grisby's place in California was hit and his two star dolphins released. Grisby got the insurance money and used that to open Cetacean Park here. That's the missing piece of the second puzzle, which helps solve the first puzzle."

"What piece is that?"

"Most people can't tell one dolphin from another, can they?"

"Most people don't know what to look for."

"But Sanders knew."

"Me, too. Misty has a pink belly and a nick in her fluke—"

"Go on the Internet, kiddo. Find Undersea World in California. Dig up newspaper stories about the raid, old websites, anything that'll have pictures of Grisby's dolphins. If the two headliners aren't doubles for Spunky and Misty, I'll eat a can of tuna without opening the can."

"You're saying Mr. Grisby *stole* his own dolphins?"

"I'm betting the ALM never hit Undersea World. Sanders figured that out but paid Grisby's insurance claim anyway."

"Why would he do that?"

"So he could blackmail Grisby. For a while, Sanders probably took cash. Then he demanded Spunky and Misty. He'd make it look like another ALM raid. Grisby can't refuse. But he plans his own double-cross, to keep the dolphins and get out from under the blackmail. He knows when the raid is coming. All he has to do is kill Sanders and claim self-defense."

"Wow. That's totally devious. Can you prove it, Uncle Steve?"

"Not a word. Not yet, anyway. You have any ideas?"

"Only one," Bobby said. "If Mr. Grisby trained Spunky and Misty to come back to the park, that's where they've got to be now."

SOLOMON'S LAWS

11. If you can't keep a promise to a loved one, you probably aren't going to keep the loved one, either.

Thirty-six

THE OFFICE FLOW CHART

"Didn't I talk to you an hour ago?" Agent Parsons sounded irritated.

"I just figured out what Grisby did," Steve said. "Actually, my nephew helped a lot, but he always lets me take the credit."

Steve pulled into a parking spot on Ponce de Leon Boulevard. He was meeting Victoria and Bobby for dinner in ten minutes. But Agent Parsons had given him her cell phone number, and now he told her his theory about Grisby's double-cross.

"Grisby has a building he calls 'the infirmary.' It's an oversize quonset hut, out of sight behind some palm trees. It has a big dolphin tank with a spillway into the channel. Bobby says that's got to be where he's keeping the dolphins. If you get a search warrant and a squad of marshals, we can hit the place tonight."

"Now? Saturday night?"

"What's the matter, they don't pay you overtime?"

"I don't have the authority to seek a search warrant on a Wednesday morning, much less call a federal judge at home on a Saturday night. I need to speak to my superiors."

"Fine. Do it now."

"And just what crime am I supposedly investigating?"

"Murder, for starters. Grisby assassinated Sanders."

"No federal jurisdiction. You know that, Solomon."

"How about insurance fraud?"

"Outside the scope of my investigation. I'm not after the fish-park guy."

Steve didn't take the time to explain that dolphins aren't fish. "What are you, a salesclerk at Macy's? This isn't your department?"

"We have procedures, Solomon. We have an office flow chart."

"That's why people hate the government. And department stores."

"Relax, Solomon. First thing Monday morning, I'll bring it up in a staff meeting. Don't bother me till then."

The phone clicked off just as Steve called her a word that rhymes with "rich."

A moment later, Victoria pulled into the parking spot in front of him, swinging her Mini Cooper to the curb without having to back up. She got out of the car, and Steve waited for the passenger door to open. But it didn't.

Where's Bobby?

* * *

"Bobby said you wanted him to stay off his feet," Victoria told Steve. "Something about tomorrow's game."

"I didn't mean he shouldn't come to dinner."

They were seated at a corner table in Restaurant St. Michel, a romantic dining spot in a 1920's hotel. A pianist played "I've Got You Under My Skin," and diners whispered to one another in the elegant art deco room. Steve figured that Victoria, consistent to her core, would order sugarcane skewered pork tenderloin with a rum molasses glaze. She wouldn't touch the grilled pineapple plantain chips, so he would clean off her plate along with his filet mignon tartar. Bobby loved the crab cakes, so it puzzled Steve that his nephew hadn't come along.

"What was Bobby doing when you left?" he asked.

"Eating a cheese sandwich and working on the computer."

Steve made a *hmm*-ing sound.

"What are you worried about?" she asked.

"I'm not sure."

"I told Bobby we'd be home early and we'd bring him dessert."

"What'd he ask for? Tiramisu or key lime pie?"

"Neither. He said he didn't want to overload on sugar."

Steve thought that over. Maybe the boy was just worried about the game. "I told Bobby he was pitching, and I think it scared him a little."

"How'd you get Ira Kreindler to let Bobby pitch?"

"I haven't yet, but I'll persuade him."

"How? You know what a hardhead he is."

"You still have that gun Pincher gave you?"

"I'm serious, Steve. You shouldn't get Bobby's hopes up if you can't deliver."

"I never make a promise to you or Bobby that I can't keep."

"What bothers me are the methods you use to keep those promises."

"Let's not fight about it. Let's eat and get home, so I can talk to Bobby."

Victoria picked up the menu and studied it.

"I'll eat your pineapple chips," Steve offered.

"I'm not ordering pork tenderloin. I'm getting the yellowtail snapper with the curry sauce."

"Oh."

"Don't look so disappointed. You can order pineapple chips on the side."

"It's not that. You're becoming less predictable."

"Is that a bad thing?"

"I don't know."

"People grow, Steve. They change."

"They become prosecutors."

"Don't start on that. Now, tell me everything that happened today."

"I thought I already had."

"You gave me bits and pieces. Start at the beginning."

Steve did as he was told. It had been an eventful day.

Mai Ling leading him to FBI Agent Constance Parsons.

Agent Parsons turning out to be Nash's girlfriend Passion Conner.

Sanders meeting with Grisby two days before the raid and likely blackmailing him long before that.

Parsons letting the raid go ahead in order to nail Hardcastle.

Bobby figuring out that Grisby still had the dolphins.

Victoria listened attentively. Unlike Steve, she seldom interrupted. She liked to vacuum up every bit of information and process it a moment or two before responding. This time a glass of California wine helped the processing. A Sangiovese from Eberle Winery. Victoria said it tasted of cherry cola and raspberries, with a hint of licorice. Steve thought it tasted like a damn good Chianti; but then, he was no expert.

"Look at all of Grisby's connections to Sanders," Steve said, summing up. "The first insurance claim. Sanders showing up at Cetacean Park just before the raid. Grisby lying in wait for him with a shotgun. I'll bet I can find a money trail from Grisby to Sanders, proving the blackmail and furnishing the motive for murder."

"What about those two guys from Hardcastle, the ones in the Lincoln?"

"Yeah? What about them?"

"Grisby double-crossed them, too, right?"

"Sure. They thought Sanders had it all worked out with Grisby. Make it look like an animal rights attack and haul the dolphins away in the confusion."

Victoria signaled the waiter for a refill on the wine. "So, if Bobby figured that the dolphins are back at the park, wouldn't those two guys figure the same thing?"

Thirty-seven

RISKING IT ALL FOR LOVE

Steve knew.

The lights were on in their house, but pulling into the driveway, he knew.

As he walked toward the front door, Victoria pulled up in her car.

Steve unlocked the door and called out Bobby's name. No answer.

Steve knew the house was empty.

He knew that Bobby's bicycle would be gone, too.

He knew that Bobby was headed for Cetacean Park. He just didn't know how long a head start the boy had.

* * *

The wind was in Bobby's face. Riding over the bridge to Key Biscayne always took longer than riding back to the mainland because the wind came off the ocean. Tonight, it wasn't bad. Warm and moist, the breeze like a washcloth.

Bobby had left the house just after Victoria drove off to meet Uncle Steve for dinner. Now it was dark, a half-moon was rising over the Bay, and he pulled his bicycle into a strand of scrubby pine trees adjacent to Cetacean Park.

Uncle Steve had let him down again. Two hours ago Bobby told his uncle that Spunky and Misty had to be back at the park. That's the only thing that made sense. His uncle promised to do something about it. Then he called back later. He said the FBI would get on it Monday.

Monday!

Right now, Grisby could be loading Spunky and Misty into tanks for transport. Just like he'd done before when he'd brought the dolphins from California. Bobby had found photographs of Undersea World. The shots of Spunky were difficult to make out, a lot of water splashing. But one photo of Misty was unmistakable. The little notch in her fluke and her pink belly gave her away.

Bobby imagined what might be going on right now at Cetacean Park. Those two men from Hardcastle could be there. Pissed off at the double-cross. Ready to kill Grisby. Kidnap the dolphins, sneak them off to the warfare center in San Diego, turn them into freaks and assassins.

My best buds.

This was his only chance, or they'd be gone forever. Didn't Uncle Steve say that men always did whatever had to be done, no matter the risk? Especially for those you love.

Well, I love Spunky and Misty, and I'm their only hope.

Bobby worked his way to the dock, listening to the whisper of water in the channel. No dolphins. He wondered what time Uncle Steve and Victoria would get home. They'd be hacked off. But it wasn't his fault.

Uncle Steve should have gotten the dolphins back, or at least he should have tried harder. *But he was so caught up trying to prove his stupid client innocent, he forgot about the dolphins . . . and about me.*

"Family comes first." That's what he'd always said. But he was still a lawyer, and Bobby sensed a conflict between obligations to the family you love and the scumbags you represent.

A splash in the channel, but it was just a small fish leaping, the moonlight catching its phosphorescence. No Spunky. No Misty.

Bobby followed the channel toward the main building. During the day, a busy place, with a souvenir stand, a food court, and a dolphin video playing on a flat screen. Growing more narrow, the channel wound inland past the building under an umbrella of leafy palms. It ended at a spillway that came from the quonset hut Mr. Grisby called "the infirmary."

The building was thirty feet high, made of corrugated metal. The roof was elevated by wooden rafters, leaving an open breezeway that ran the circumference of the round building. Bobby could see lights through the breezeway, and he could hear men's voices.

He climbed a ladder that ran up the side of the building. Halfway up, Bobby recognized Mr. Grisby's voice, but couldn't make out the words. Then a shrill metal whistle. Bobby knew the sound. Mr. Grisby trained dolphins with blasts from a whistle.

The ladder stopped at a metal catwalk just at the breezeway. By standing on his tiptoes, Bobby could see down into the building. There was Mr. Grisby, on a platform no wider than a diving board. Two men stood at the perimeter of the tank. A smaller man in cowboy boots and a black T-shirt. Tough-looking dude. And a larger man with blond hair, muscles not as well defined.

Mr. Grisby tooted the whistle and Spunky and Misty jumped in unison, landed, then paddled upright on their flukes, looking like ballerinas.

"Watch this, gentlemen. I think you'll be impressed."

Grisby knelt down and grabbed a large nylon sack that lay at his feet. He opened the drawstrings, and something tumbled out of the sack and into the water.

A body in a green-and-brown camouflage uniform.

Thirty-eight

STRIDE FOR STRIDE

"Shit."

Steve slammed the heel of his hand against the steering wheel.

From the top of the bridge, nothing but twin rows of red taillights in front of them. At the bottom of the span, two police cars and a tow truck blocked the eastbound lane. A Hummer sat diagonally in the roadway, a deep-hulled sailboat splintered across the lanes, where it had fallen off its trailer.

"What now?" Victoria asked.

"We walk. Or run. C'mon."

Steve pulled the car as far off the roadway as he could, and they started on foot. A jog at first. They'd both changed clothes after dinner. Victoria was in her workout attire: Nike stretch pants, running shoes, and fitted top. Steve wore khaki shorts and an old Hurricanes baseball jersey.

Once off the bridge, they were able to cut through the picnic areas that lined the causeway, just yards from the shoreline. Their path was lit by hundreds of headlights from the traffic jam. White gulls trudged along the beach, digging for toenail crabs.

"This is all my fault," Steve said as they jogged alongside each other.

"What is?"

"Bobby. I've been too self-absorbed. I haven't paid enough attention to him."

"You're a wonderful father to him, Steve. Bobby adores you."

"I haven't been consistent. At first, because of everything he'd suffered with my crazy sister, I didn't want to deny him anything. Then I thought maybe I was overprotecting him, so I backed off. Now I just don't know. I've lost all sense of balance."

"All parents learn on the fly, and you're doing fine."

"If I were doing so great, he'd be home right now." Steve shot a look across the Bay in the direction of Cetacean Park. "If anything happens to him..."

His words hung in the humid air, and they ran in silence for another few moments.

Just after they'd left the house, Steve had called FBI Agent Parsons again on her cell. This time, she sounded even more exasperated. "Your twelve-year-old nephew has ridden off on his bicycle, and you think it's a federal case? Is that it, Solomon?"

She hung up on him.

Next, Steve called the Miami Police Department and got through to a desk sergeant. When it became clear that Bobby hadn't been snatched, and that he'd been gone less than two hours, Steve could feel the officer's interest level wane. Following procedures, the sergeant said to call back in the morning if the boy hadn't returned.

"Do you know what first attracted me to you?" Victoria said as they neared the collapsed trailer and sailboat.

"My musk cologne?"

"Your love for Bobby. The risks you took to rescue him. The way you put him first. With all your faults, you're still the kind of man a woman wants to father her children."

"What faults?"

"C'mon, Steve. Let's pick up the pace."

They broke into a full run, Steve shortening his stride just a bit to match hers. Victoria ran athletically, smoothly. They were in perfect rhythm, perfect sync, and moving fast.

They passed cars parked at water's edge on the causeway's lover's lane. Couples inside. Drinking. Kissing. Writhing. Close by, a homeless man with a scrawny dog rummaged through a trash barrel.

The tow truck was still there in the middle of the roadway, where they'd first seen it from the top of the bridge. Workers were trying figure out how to hoist the sailboat off the pavement.

The causeway eased toward the right, and the warm southeast sea breeze hit them head-on. Behind them, horns honked, and traffic still hadn't moved. They could see the lights of Cetacean Park, less than a mile ahead.

Steve gestured toward Victoria's purse, a black leather Dolce & Gabbana. "Isn't that slowing you down?"

"A woman never leaves her purse in the car."

"You want me to carry it?"

"No way. You're not licensed."

Steve gave her a look that she took as a question. It was the second time that night he'd asked.

"Yes," Victoria said. "I still have the gun Pincher gave me."

Thirty-nine

DEAD DUMMY

It wasn't a body.

It was a dummy. Like the ones used by the Navy in rescue training.

Bobby climbed over the low wall and watched from high in the rafters. Wedged against a beam, he was hidden in the shadows, his head bumping against the corrugated metal ceiling.

Spunky and Misty were somewhere deep in the tank below. The dummy floated faceup. Mr. Grisby held two wooden sticks that looked like pool cues, only shorter. The man in cowboy boots and the larger man watched as Mr. Grisby clacked the sticks together three times. A second later, both dolphins burst from the water. Spunky grabbed the dummy by an ankle and dived, dragging it with him. Misty stayed on the surface, turning circles, as if on surveillance.

The seconds passed. A minute. Two minutes. If the dummy had been a man, he'd be turning blue. After three minutes, Mr. Grisby blew the whistle. Again, Spunky blasted through the surface, this time tossing the dummy onto the platform, splashing the three men.

A good way to kill an enemy saboteur, Bobby thought.

Or Rich (The Shit) Shactman.

Mr. Grisby reached into a pail and tossed chunks of raw fish to each of the dolphins. Misty shot water out of her blowhole and made a *click-click* sound that Bobby knew meant "thanks." Spunky's sound was more whiny, the thanks combined with a sound meaning he was still hungry.

"Nice party trick," Cowboy Boots said.

"But I'm not sure it's worth a million bucks," the larger man said. "We can train the bastards, too."

"Even without Sanders?"

Their voices carried easily across the water and echoed up the metal walls.

"Big deal. We hire another frogman," Cowboy Boots said.

"The home office is none too happy with you about the whole Sanders deal," the other man said.

"I'm telling you," Grisby said, "Sanders was working for the feds. He was trying to arrest me when I shot him."

"Bullshit," Cowboy Boots said.

"If Sanders was a snitch, you'd have been busted instead of that dipshit kid," the other man added. "Anyway, you got no cause to double the price on us. There's a place in the Dominican we can go. Six dolphins trained to B level."

Grisby laughed. "Try to get a B level to do this."

He kicked the dummy back into the water, then rattled the two sticks against each other like a drummer in a marching band. He kept the *rat-a-tat-tat* going until Spunky and Misty each grabbed the dummy by an ankle. They swam in opposite directions, whipping their bodies in a violent pitch and roll. The dummy tore in half cleanly at the crotch. Each dolphin shook its head and tossed half the dead dummy onto the platform.

"Jesus," Cowboy Boots muttered.

Grisby grinned at the two men. "Either of you want to take a swim?"

The big man laughed nervously. "We'll get back to you on the price. We got to talk to the home office."

Grisby tossed two pieces of mackerel to the dolphins, who were standing on their fluttering flukes, waving their fins, as if applauding themselves.

Wedged into his hiding place, Bobby felt himself tremble. Were these his best buddies?

What have they done to you?

The dolphins began leaping. Competing to see who could jump higher. Spunky was bigger and stronger, but Misty had a sleeker body. On their third leap, they neared the rafters. At the apogee of her jump, Misty stared straight at Bobby. She hung motionless in the air for a fraction of a second and emitted a *toot* through her blowhole. Not her usual greeting. Bobby translated the sound as an urgent and fearful, *"Stranger."*

Both dolphins curved gracefully back into the water below. Five seconds later, they shot toward him again, even closer this time. They whistled in unison. *"Stranger!"* The tone was frightening, the meaning of the word even more so.

Have they brainwashed you? Have they turned me into a stranger?

Once back in the water, the dolphins swam in a circle, splashing the men on the platform.

Stop it, guys! Are you trying to blow my cover?

"Something's got 'em riled." Cowboy Boots looked toward the rafters, shielding his eyes from the glare of the overhead lights.

"Probably just some bats," Grisby said.

Bobby squeezed his eyes shut. He harbored the irrational thought that if he couldn't see the men, they couldn't see him. He tried to press himself even farther into the joint of the two beams. A second later, Spunky leapt from the water, his dorsal fin swiping Bobby's leg. Startled, Bobby's foot slipped off the beam. He fell, one foot on each side of the rafter. Landed hard on his private parts, howled with pain.

"What the hell's that!" Cowboy Boots yelled.

All three men looked straight up, squinting into the lights.

"Who's up there!" Grisby demanded.

Bobby felt like a horse had kicked him in the balls. The pain was so intense, it blinded him. Feeling nauseous, he slid backward on his butt along the rafter, a narrow two-by-four.

From below, he heard a frightening sound. The *clickety-clack* of a shotgun racking.

"I said, who's up there! Last chance, or I'll fill you with buckshot."

Dizzy now, Bobby lost his balance and flipped over. He hung upside down from the beam by his ankles, as if on monkey bars.

"What the hell's that?" The larger man pointed toward the rafters.

Bobby's thighs ached. He tried swinging upright on the beam but didn't have the strength.

He teetered left.

Teetered right.

He was losing his grip, and the building seemed to tilt on its axis.

A second later, he plunged into the water, surprised at how cold it felt, how salty it tasted. A second after that, something grabbed him by one ankle.

Forty

DOLPHIN LOVE

Spunky spun Bobby in the tank, whirling him around and around. His shirt tore, and his shorts were dragged down to his knees. Spunky sped up, Bobby spinning so fast his eyes blurred and his sinuses filled with water.

If it were Chanukah, he'd be a human dreidel.

Mr. Grisby blasted his whistle and Spunky let go. The rafters continued twirling above Bobby's head, looking like wooden horses on a carousel. He choked on the salt water, then upchucked all over himself.

"Who the hell is that?" Cowboy Boots snarled.

"Robert Solomon," Mr. Grisby said. "You've already met his uncle."

"That lawyer. Oh, shit."

"How much did you hear, Robert?"

"Nothing." Bobby treaded water. "Nothing at all."

"He's lying," the big man said. "It's like a drum in here."

"Either way," Grisby said, "he's seen the dolphins. He's seen the two of you."

"I lost my glasses. I can't see anything. Really, Mr. Grisby."

Pleading, Bobby knew. Pleading for his life. He didn't have any other ideas.

"What are you gonna do, Grisby?" the big man said.

Mr. Grisby picked up the two sticks. "One more demo for you to tell your bosses about. It'll prove the total discipline of my training."

"How so?"

"The dolphins know Robert. They like him. But properly trained dolphins are one hundred percent obedient. They're deprived of free will."

"The Manchurian dolphin?" the big man asked. "That what you saying?"

"Just watch. They'll do to the boy the same thing they did that dummy."

"No, Mr. Grisby!" Bobby could picture himself being ripped in two, his intestines spewing out into the water like links of sausage.

Misty circled Bobby, her fin brushing his arms. Spunky made a sound through his blowhole. The same rhythmic beats as before. *"Stranger."* But this time, the dolphin turned his beak toward the platform. He pointed toward Mr. Grisby. It took Bobby a moment to figure out the message. He'd gotten it wrong before.

I'm not the stranger. Mr. Grisby has become a stranger to them.

They're warning me.

Thanks, but it's a little late.

Bobby put two fingers to his mouth and whistled a singsong: *"I love you."*

Mr. Grisby started rattling the sticks together. It was the cue for each dolphin to grab an ankle and begin tearing him apart.

Neither one obeyed. Instead, Misty grabbed Bobby by the shoulder, her mouth gentle, her teeth not even breaking the skin. She held him upright in the water, letting him rest. No more need to keep pedaling to stay afloat.

Grisby banged the sticks again, harder.

Misty held Bobby still, rustling the water with her fluke.

"Goddammit!" Grisby fumed. "Follow orders." He blew into his whistle. A shrill, piercing sound.

Spunky dived, leaving Misty on the surface, still holding Bobby by the shoulder.

"What the hell's wrong with you two?" Grisby shouted.

Bobby looked at Misty, heard her *click-click*. The word "breathe."

She's waiting for me. She's waiting for me to take a deep breath.

Bobby exhaled. He took the deepest breath he could. Then Misty dived, carrying the boy straight to the bottom of the fifteen-foot tank.

Bobby could hear Grisby screaming cuss words as they went under.

Spunky was already there, working his beak on the metal handle of a grated door that led to the spillway. The handle, a sliding bolt, wouldn't budge. Maybe it was rusted. Maybe the water pressure was just too strong. Despite his great strength, Spunky seemed stymied.

Bobby was running out of breath.

He exhaled a burst, felt his lungs tighten.

Spunky swam backwards, got a running start, swung sideways, and banged his bulk into the steal door, snapping the bolt. He pushed against the door with his beak, swinging it open.

Bobby knew he was drowning.

Misty tightened her grip on Bobby's shoulder. She carried him through the door and into the spillway. Spunky came behind, nudging at Bobby's feet. The three of them picked up speed with the flow of the water, and emerged at the bottom of the spillway and into the channel. Misty pulled Bobby to the surface, and the boy felt the night air. He gobbled half a dozen fast breaths and hung on to Misty's dorsal fin. Behind them, Bobby heard the endless blasts of Mr. Grisby's whistle.

* * *

Steve chugged to a stop under a palm tree a few hundred yards from the channel. They were at the edge of the park. He stood, hunched over, hands on hips, sucking air. Victoria breathed normally. Was she even sweating? An hour on the treadmill each day and singles tennis under the Florida sun will build your endurance.

"You're not even winded," Steve said. Sounded peeved.

"You have to learn to pace yourself."

"What are you talking about?"

"Life's a marathon. You can't burn yourself out."

Steve straightened up and looked around. The channel was quiet. A half-moon gave off a soft glow, and the palm fronds rustled in the warm breeze. He looked past the bend in the channel, toward the quonset building, where light shone through the breezeway.

"Someone's in there," he said, pointing.

Before they'd taken two steps, a shrill sound came from the direction of the building. A whistle. One long bleat, followed by numerous short blasts.

SOLOMON'S LAWS

12. Life may be a marathon, but sometimes you have to sprint to save a life.

Forty-one

SHOOT THE LAWYER

Bobby heard the whistle and the shouts behind them. Mr. Grisby and the two men. They'd raced out of the building and were on the dock. Then the sound of a motor. A Jet Ski firing up.

The dolphins picked up speed, heading toward the channel gate, Spunky leading the way, Bobby riding on top of Misty.

But why go there?

The gate would be locked. There was no escape.

Behind them, a shotgun blast. Riding the Jet Ski, Grisby fired a shot into the air. Bobby winced. The dolphins kept swimming. Not even a shudder.

* * *

At the sound of the shotgun blast, Steve and Victoria stopped short.

"What the hell!"

They heard the roar of the Jet Ski and raced toward the embankment. Fifty yards away, they were stunned to see Bobby fly by on the back of a dolphin.

"Bobby!"

But he didn't hear his uncle.

Close behind was Grisby on a Jet Ski, a shotgun slung over his shoulder. Steve took off along the channel, just as he had when chasing Nash. This time, he ran even faster, his feet barely touching the scrubby weeds growing out of the sand. He felt strong, focused. He knew the distance to the gate, knew the shortcut, knew just what he would do.

He'd jumped the channel before. He'd knocked Nash ass-over-elbows.

He would do the same thing to Grisby.

"Wait up!" Victoria yelled, running after him.

But Steve couldn't wait. *Sure, Vic, life is a marathon. But sometimes, to save a life, you gotta sprint.*

* * *

Misty leapt from the water, splashed down again, Bobby hanging on with both hands around her neck. Spunky swam just ahead, leading them.

The gate was a hundred yards away. From water level, it looked impossibly high. Maybe ten feet above the waterline, with another two feet of razor wire on top. Nasty.

Could the dolphins jump it? Bobby didn't know. They'd never tried. If they jumped, would they be chopped to pieces on the razor wire, along with him?

The dolphins slowed. They weren't going to jump. They were going to stop at the gate. Through her blowhole, Misty bleated one word. *"Go!"*

It took him a second to figure it out. Misty would stop at the gate and let Bobby stand on her back. The gate was a series of vertical metal bars attached top and bottom to two horizontal bars. Skinny as he was, he could work himself through the vertical bars to get into the Bay. Swim from there to the causeway, and safety. Spunky and Misty would stay behind. They would sacrifice themselves to save him.

Bobby clicked a *"No, no, no"* to Misty. Then, *"Faster!"*

Behind them, the roar of the Jet Ski grew louder.

Bobby smacked Misty's flank and whistled a command. *"We jump!"*

Misty picked up speed. Powerboat fast, churning up a foamy wake.

The gate was fifty yards away.

The Jet Ski bounced in the dolphins' wake. Grisby slung the shotgun into firing position.

* * *

Steve ran full bore along the channel.

He watched Bobby clinging to the dolphin, nearing the locked gate.

And there was Grisby, closing the distance on the Jet Ski, swinging the shotgun off his shoulder.

Bobby rubbed Misty near her blowhole as they neared the gate. Shouting now. "Jump! Jump, Misty! Jump!"

The dolphin launched herself out of the water, Bobby hanging on to her dorsal fin, like a cowboy on a bucking bronco.

Grisby lifted the shotgun. He aimed it squarely in the middle of Bobby's back.

Steve reached the embankment, and launched himself toward Grisby.

Grisby sensed the movement and swung the shotgun from the hip, as if intending to drop a grouse from the sky. Before he could pull the trigger, Spunky blasted from beneath the water, and smacked Grisby flush across the face with his powerful fluke. Grisby's neck

shot back with an audible crack, and he tumbled off
the Jet Ski. Steve belly-flopped into the water. Next to
him, Grisby floated on his back, his eyes open, but his
face expressionless.

Misty cleared the gate, sailing over the razor wire
with room to spare. Bobby tumbled over Misty's dorsal fin, landing face-first in the water. Spunky leapt the
gate a moment later and joined them in the open Bay.

"Come back here, kid!"

It was Cowboy Boots, on the embankment, pointing a handgun into the darkness of the Bay. The larger
man was alongside. They'd ridden a golf cart along the
path to the gate.

"Keep going, Bobby!" Steve shouted, treading water in the channel.

"Shoot the lawyer!" the larger man ordered.

Cowboy Boots fired two rounds into the water in
Steve's direction. "Get those animals to come back,
kid. If you don't, I'll kill your uncle."

"Drop that gun," a woman's voice ordered, "or I'll
put a hole in the back of your stupid head."

Cowboy Boots didn't move. He didn't drop the gun,
either.

"She'll do it," Steve said, treading water. "She's shot
lots of stupid men."

Cowboy Boots seemed to think it over.

Victoria pulled back the hammer on her state-issued
.38. An ominous *click*.

Cowboy Boots dropped his handgun.

"Turn around slowly, both of you," Victoria ordered.

The men did as they were told. Suddenly, the bigger
man reached behind his back and pulled something
out of his waistband.

A second gun.

Victoria fired.

The round zinged by the big man's head, and he dropped the gun, along with what smelled suspiciously like a load in his pants.

Above them, the *chockety-chock* of engines. A helicopter descended; a powerful searchlight swept the channel and the embankment. A sharpshooter with a scoped rifle leaned out the open door. Next to him, FBI Agent Constance Parsons yelled into a bullhorn: "Everyone freeze!"

Forty-two

CRIME SCENE

It took hours. There were stories to tell and retell to dozens of cops, investigators, and agents.

City of Miami. Miami-Dade Sheriff's Office. FBI. U.S. Marshal. Village of Key Biscayne, highly useful for directing traffic on the causeway.

Cop cars, flashing lights, crackling radios. Photographers, Forensics guys and gals, and a camera crew from Channel 4. No one from the *Miami Herald* was there, the newspaper having cut its staff so severely, it now took a triple homicide or Fidel Castro's gallbladder to make it into the paper.

Three paramedics vehicles came to the park, but they only needed one. Wade Grisby was loaded onto a backboard, his neck packed in ice. The ambulance whisked him off to Jackson Memorial, Steve hearing whispers of "broken neck" and "paralysis."

Bobby refused to come out of the water until a cop paddled over in an inflatable and used a tire iron to break the lock on the channel gate. The cop swung the gate open, Bobby *click-clack*ed some message to Spunky and Misty, who headed back up the channel, the cop closing the gate behind them.

Ray Pincher relieved Victoria of her gun, telling her that in the half century Assistant State Attorneys had been issued handguns, none had ever been fired at a suspect. Victoria asked if she'd done anything wrong. No, Pincher told her. But he was still taking the gun. The case against Nash would be dismissed and her duties would officially end at five P.M. Monday.

The two guys turned out to be Larry Vollman, who now needed a change of underwear, and Richard Zinn, Mr. Cowboy Boots. They ran Wellfleet Investigations, which, though buried under two or three layers of corporate paperwork, was a distant cousin of Hardcastle Energy Services. After three cups of coffee and a flashlight beam in the face, they yapped for an hour.

"We didn't do anything wrong."

"Sanders told us we had a deal to buy the dolphins from Grisby."

"It had to look like an animal rights raid, but that was none of our business."

"We just do what Hardcastle tells us."

"Sure, we'll give you our boss's name, and anything else you need."

Paramedics wrapped Steve and Bobby in blankets, checked their vital signs, and pronounced them healthy. Bobby talked up a storm to Agent Parsons, asking what would happen to Spunky and Misty. She promised to look into it.

"Not good enough," Steve said.

"I beg your pardon." Agent Parsons' tone was not begging in the least.

"You're too busy. You'll never get around to it."

"Maybe not today, but—"

"The dolphins have to be fed. They have to be cared for. We know a place in Key Largo with great facilities.

They bring in kids from hospitals to swim with the dolphins. I can have the owners up here in twelve hours."

"Then what do you need from me?"

"I just don't want some U.S. Marshal blocking our way, claiming those dolphins are evidence or government property or whatever bullshit red tape they come up with."

"I'll get the clearance you need in the morning. Fair enough?"

"Deal."

Around dawn, a lunch truck pulled up. One of the chrome-paneled wagons that service construction sites. Sandwiches, chips, and sodas were passed around.

Steve's cell phone was water-logged, so he borrowed Victoria's phone, and with Ray Pincher's help, he got through to the jail.

"Your lawyer wants to talk to you, but first I gotta apologize," Pincher said when Gerald Nash was on the line. "I'm sorry I charged you with murder. But you're still a horse's ass, and so's your old man."

The apology apparently having been accepted, Pincher cracked his knuckles and handed Steve the phone.

"Good news, Gerald," Steve told him. "They're gonna let you out in a couple hours, so I want to wish you good luck."

"Thanks, man. You've been great."

"Ordinarily, I'd come over there, help you with the paperwork, but I've got a prior commitment. So if it's okay with you..."

"That's cool, Solomon."

"You have any plans, Gerald?"

"Heading to Denmark, as soon as I can."

"Denmark?"

"Most of the world's mink farms are there. There's work to be done."

"You take care, Gerald."

"Say, is Passion with you?"

"Agent Parsons? Yeah, but she's kind of busy right now."

"Tell her I don't hold grudges. If she wants to go to Denmark..."

Steve said good-bye and checked on Bobby, who was still yakking with any cop who was interested. Victoria came by, wrapped her arms around Steve, and whispered, "You were right this time, lover."

"Wild guess about Grisby. His story never felt right. I'm just happy we saved Bobby's pals."

"What about going up against me in court? You seem to enjoy pulling my chain."

"Well, it does rev my engine. Speaking of which, do you realize how long it's been since we...?"

"After Bobby's game today. Okay?"

"The game! Jeez, what time is it?"

Before Victoria could answer, Steve spotted Constance Parsons standing inside a minyan of *federales*. "Agent Parsons! We've got an emergency here."

"What now?" she asked.

"Your helicopter. We need it."

Forty-three

PLAY BALL

There are many ways to get to a Sunday school league baseball game at Sunniland Park in Kendall. Easiest is to drive down Dixie Highway. Metrorail works, too, if you bring a bicycle along for the last leg of the trip.

But today, Bobby, Steve, and Victoria took an FBI helicopter. The chopper ferried them from Key Biscayne, across the Bay, to Coconut Grove, Bobby silently watching the still, turquoise water in the morning sun. His eyes were distant, baseball surely not on his mind.

"They're gonna be okay, kiddo," Steve said.

"I know."

"We'll go down to Key Largo a lot. When the kids from the hospital come by, you'll introduce them to Spunky and Misty."

"Can I teach the kids to talk dolphinese?"

"You bet."

The water below them was shallow and clear, brown sea grasses waving below the surface.

"I'm sorry about all that stuff that happened before, Uncle Steve."

"What stuff?"

Bobby shrugged, and the helicopter passed over the

shoreline of Coconut Grove, following the path of banyan trees along Main Highway.

"You know. All the mean things I said about you not caring about Spunky and Misty."

"Not a problem, kiddo. You were upset."

"Yeah. But that's not an excuse. It was extremely..." He paused to dig up a word. "...immature of me."

"You're a Solomon. Immaturity is expected from time to time. Now, are you ready to take the mound?"

"Coach Kreindler won't let me pitch in a real game."

"We'll see."

The helicopter landed at the neighborhood park on Morningside Drive, where a police car met them and drove Bobby the few blocks to the house on Kumquat. He changed into his Beth Am Bobcats uniform, grabbed his glove and spikes, and the cops brought him back to the helicopter. They took off again, and seven minutes later, the chopper with the FBI logo was settling into the outfield, where the Bobcats and the Bashers were finishing warm-ups.

Now, that's what I call making an entrance, Steve thought.

Bobby, Steve, and Victoria hopped out.

"Go warm up that throwing arm," Steve told Bobby, who raced off to join his teammates.

Coach Ira Kreindler waddled out of dugout, waving his arms.

"What's the meaning of this!" Kreindler huffed to a stop near second base.

"We're delivering your starting pitcher." Steve gave the pilot the thumbs-up, and the FBI chopper lifted off.

Kreindler hung onto his yarmulke in the wind from the rotors. "Forget it, Solomon. I've got enough problems today."

He thrust a lineup card into Steve's hand. Penciled in as the leadoff hitter for the First Baptist Bashers was "R. Schactman."

"Richie on the Bashers?" Steve said. "I don't get it."

"That spoiled *momzer* switched teams. He said the scouts from Gulliver and Ransom would see him play more on a better team."

"What a bastard," Steve agreed.

"So forget about Robert pitching. The ball Shactman hit off him in practice hasn't come down yet. Besides, Robert missed warm-ups, and you know my rules. If you're late, you don't play."

Victoria intervened in her customary, polite way. "Mr. Kreindler, couldn't you make an exception? Bobby's had an incredibly hard night."

"Yeah, Kreindler," Steve said. "While you were making chopped liver, he caught a murderer and two thugs and rescued two endangered dolphins."

Kreindler gave them a dubious look that made Steve want to punch him in the throat. "I'm sure he did, but rules are rules."

"Like the kosher rules?" Victoria asked. "What are they called?"

"The kashruth, Ms. Lord. That happens to be my business. Kreindler's Kosher Meats."

"My business is enforcing the law, at least until I turn in my badge tomorrow. Are you aware it's consumer fraud to sell nonkosher food as kosher?"

"How dare you!"

"One word from me, and the State Attorney's Office will launch an investigation."

"That's ridiculous. I've never sold a milligram of *trayf* in my life."

"Then an investigation will clear you. In two or three months."

Steve laughed. "That's a lot of rotting brisket."

"Ms. Lord, I never expected this from you."

"Me, either," Steve said. "Vic, you're terrific. You're outstanding. You're—"

"An extortionist!" Kreindler fumed.

"Just let Bobby pitch two innings," she suggested.

"That's all anyone can pitch! League rules."

"Good. It's settled, then. And, of course, I'll be so busy tomorrow, I won't have time to open any new investigations."

Kreindler's face turned the color of borscht. "You've got some chutzpah, lady." He sighed so heavily, his throat wattles waffled.

*　*　*

Bobby took his warm-up pitches while Rich Shactman, the traitor, glared at him from the on-deck circle.

Concentrate, Bobby told himself. Keep the ball under control. Remember everything Uncle Steve taught you.

"Imagine a circle where you want to put the pitch, and paint everything else black. You won't see the batter. You won't see anything but that circle."

Rich Shactman stepped into the batter's box and crowded the plate, daring Bobby to pitch inside. He pointed his bat at the pitcher's mound and squeezed one eye shut as if sighting a rifle. "Right back at you, Word Boy."

Bobby turned toward the bleachers where Uncle Steve and Victoria were nestled together, their shoulders touching. Bobby nodded to indicate he was okay. He wasn't going to pee his pants just because Rich the Shit Shactman was twirling a Louisville Slugger at him.

Behind the plate, catcher Miguel Juarez signaled for a fast ball inside. Bobby focused his mind, painting the circle right under Shactman's hands, trying to move the prick off the plate.

Bobby wound up, kicked high, and whipped his arm forward. A blazing fastball six inches inside hit Miguel's mitt with a *thud* that echoed across the field. Shactman staggered backward, stunned at the speed of the pitch.

"Ball one," the umpire called.

"You hit me, I'll kill you!" Shactman snarled.

Bobby shrugged like it was no big deal.

In his catcher's crouch, Miguel showed two fingers— curveball. Coach Kreindler didn't want the boys throwing curves, but there wasn't much he could do about it.

Bobby held the ball with his index and middle fingers and snapped his wrist at the moment of release. The pitch seemed to sail inside, and again Shactman stepped back, his knees buckling. But this time, the ball broke over the plate.

"Strike one!" the umpire yelled.

Shactman looked embarrassed. He'd bailed out like a sissy.

Bobby worked quickly now. Another fastball. Right over the plate. The ball had already *pop*ped into Miguel's glove by the time Shactman started his swing.

"Strike two!"

Shactman seemed bewildered. He moved deeper into the batter's box, dug his back foot into the dirt. Miguel signaled for a curve, on the outside corner. Bobby shook his head. He wanted strength against strength. Fastball against power hitter. Mano a mano. He wasn't afraid.

"Right back at *you,* Shactman," Bobby called out.

"Huh?" Shactman stared at him.

"Fastball down the pipe."

Calling his pitch, letting the prick know, challenging his manhood.

Bobby worked two fingers across the seams, resting his thumb under the ball. He wound up, lifting both elbows shoulder high. He took the drop step and rotated his hips, his arm whipping forward.

A bullet, waist high, over the dead center of the plate.

Shactman's swing was hard, but late, and it threw him off balance. Legs tangled, he collapsed in a heap.

Miguel yelled "Ouch" when the ball pounded into his mitt.

"Strike three!" The umpire punched his fist. "You're outta here."

Shactman got to his feet, dusted off his pants, and stalked toward the dugout, never returning Bobby's stare.

Bobby picked up the resin bag, squeezed it, tossed it back to the ground. He hitched up his pants, pulled at his crotch, spat on the ground. He wished he had some chewing tobacco, or at least a wad of bubble gum.

I'm a pitcher. A real pitcher.

He turned toward Uncle Steve and Victoria and winked at them. Both smiled back without doing anything embarrassing like leaping up and screaming. Bobby's mind drifted for just a moment, wondering if they'd all go to Whip 'N Dip for mint chocolate chip after the game. Then the second batter nervously approached the plate, and Bobby turned to Miguel to get the sign.

* * *

In the bleachers, Steve and Victoria held hands, squeezing tightly.

"Is that a tear in the corner of your eye?" Victoria asked.

"The wind."

"It's eighty-two degrees and humid as a wet towel. Not a breath of wind."

Steve had forced himself to remain calm when Bobby struck out Rich Shactman. He'd told Bobby how to keep his poise, and Steve intended to follow his own advice.

"When you strike somebody out, kiddo, stay cool. Act like you've done it before. Like you'll strike him out every time he comes up."

Steve struggled to keep his emotions in check. He thought of the long path Bobby had traveled. The terrified, emaciated boy in the dog cage had conquered his fears. He now stood on center stage, confident and determined. Hell, he might become the star of his team. High-fives all around, root beer and pizza for everyone after the game. The feelings welled up inside, and Steve bit down hard on his lower lip, figuring the pain would keep him from blubbering.

"You knew Bobby could do this, didn't you?" Victoria said

"I knew he had potential. He just needed some guidance."

Victoria rubbed the back of Steve's neck. "You're a wonderful teacher."

"Bobby's a quick learner. And so are you."

"Me?"

"The way you bluffed Kreindler. You're stealing my game plan."

"Am I, now?"

"It's a compliment. You've learned to wing it, to shoot from the hip."

On the pitcher's mound, Bobby had one ball and two strikes on the second batter.

"I didn't shoot from the hip," Victoria corrected Steve.

"What?"

"Kosher food violations are on file in Miami Beach City Hall. Six years ago, Kreindler was cited. Something about not draining all the blood from the meat."

"You researched him?"

She gave him the faintest hint of a smile.

"Aw, I should have known," Steve said.

"Are you disappointed? That I'm not as spontaneous as you."

"No way. It's better that we're different. Makes us an unbeatable team."

Victoria leaned over and kissed him.

They watched as Bobby threw heat, a scorching fastball, for a called strike three. Victoria applauded, as did several others in the bleachers.

"You're terrific with Bobby," Steve said.

"I love him. You know that."

"You're gonna be a terrific mother."

"When?"

"When what?"

"When will I be a terrific mother?"

"When you're married."

"When *I'm* married?"

"You know what I mean. When we're . . ." He stumbled and fumbled. "C'mon, Vic. When it's time and we're ready, then obviously, we should, you know . . ."

"No. Tell me."

"Aw, jeez."

"Just say it."

"Someday we should get . . ."

He seemed fundamentally unable to say the word that rhymes with "harried."

"Get married?" she helped out.

"What's this all about? You pushing me for a formal proposal? Something you can file at city hall with the kosher meat violations?"

"It doesn't have to be formal. Nothing in writing and you don't have to ask my mother for permission. A simple, 'Will you marry me, Vic?' would do."

Kreindler was right. Victoria had ample quantities of chutzpah. Or whatever Episcopalians call it. Moxie, maybe. She could demand a jury give her client a million bucks or her boyfriend take their relationship to the next level. All without blinking or blushing.

Steve needed to reply quickly. Any delay would be interpreted as indecisive. At the same time, he wanted to yell at the umpire who had just called a ball on a pitch that had clearly caught the outside corner of the plate, knee high.

At one time, B.V., Before Victoria, Steve had been commitment phobic. But that had changed. Not only did he deeply love Victoria, Steve considered himself the world's luckiest shyster because she loved him, too. In his mind, he could easily say the words:

"Sure, Vic, I want to spend my life with you, have children with you, knock off big verdicts with you."

What would be the harm saying it aloud?

No harm.

Didn't she yearn for the same things he did? And wouldn't it be great to hear her say so?

"Will you marry me, Vic?"

She gave him a coy little smile. "I'll think about it."

SOLOMON'S LAWS

1. Try not to piss off a cop unless you have a damn good reason . . . or a damn good lawyer.

2. The best way to hustle a case is to pretend you don't want the work.

3. When arguing with a woman who is strong, intelligent, and forthright, consider using trickery, artifice, and deceit.

4. A prosecutor's job is to build a brick wall around her case. A defense lawyer's job is to tear down the wall, or at least to paint graffiti on the damn thing.

5. Listen to bus drivers, bailiffs, and twelve-year-old boys. Some days, they all know more than you do.

6. When the testimony is too damn good, when there are no contradictions and all the potholes are filled with smooth asphalt, chances are the witness is lying.

7. A shark who can't bite is nothing but a mermaid.

8. When the woman you love is angry, it's best to give her space, time, and copious quantities of wine.

9. Be confident, but not cocky. Smile, but don't snicker. And no matter how desperate your case, never let the jurors see your fear.

10. Never sleep with a medical examiner, unless you're dead.

11. If you can't keep a promise to a loved one, you probably aren't going to keep the loved one, either.

12. Life may be a marathon, but sometimes you have to sprint to save a life.

ABOUT THE AUTHOR

PAUL LEVINE worked as a newspaper reporter and trial lawyer, practicing law for seventeen years, trying cases in state and federal courts and handling appeals at every level, including the Supreme Court, before becoming a full-time novelist and screenwriter. The winner of the John D. MacDonald fiction award, Levine is the author of the Jake Lassiter novels, which have been published in twenty-three countries. *To Speak for the Dead*, the first Lassiter novel, was a national bestseller and honored as one of the best mysteries of the year by the *Los Angeles Times*. He is also the author of *9 Scorpions*, a thriller set in the U.S. Supreme Court. *Trial & Error* is the fourth in the series that includes the bestselling *Solomon vs. Lord, The Deep Blue Alibi*, and *Kill All the Lawyers*.

He was co-creator and co–executive producer of the CBS television series *First Monday* and has written extensively for *JAG*. He lives in California, where he is at work on his next suspense novel, which Bantam will publish in 2008.

Visit his website at www.paul-levine.com.

THE SUSPENSE WILL KILL YOU....

VICTOR GISCHLER

GUN MONKEYS	$6.99/$10.99
THE PISTOL POETS	$6.99/$10.99
SUICIDE SQUEEZE	$6.99/$9.99
SHOTGUN OPERA	$6.99/$9.99

ASA LARSSON

SUN STORM
$12.00/$15.00

THE BLOOD SPILT
$22.00/$28.00

MORAG JOSS

FUNERAL MUSIC	$6.99/NCR
FEARFUL SYMMETRY	$6.99/NCR
FRUITFUL BODIES	$6.99/NCR
HALF-BROKEN THINGS	$13.00/NCR
PUCCINI'S GHOSTS	$22.00/NCR

CODY MCFADYEN

SHADOW MAN
$6.99/$8.99

THE FACE OF DEATH
$24.00/$30.00

STEPHEN BOOTH

BLIND TO THE BONES
$7.50/NCR

ONE LAST BREATH
$7.50/NCR

THE DEAD PLACE
$25.00/NCR

LISA GARDNER

THE PERFECT HUSBAND	$7.99/$11.99
THE OTHER DAUGHTER	$7.99/$11.99
THE THIRD VICTIM	$7.99/$10.99
THE NEXT ACCIDENT	$7.99/$11.99
THE SURVIVORS CLUB	$7.99/$11.99
THE KILLING HOUR	$7.99/$11.99
ALONE	$7.99/$10.99
GONE	$7.99/$10.99
HIDE	$25.00/$30.00

Ask for these titles wherever books are sold, or visit us online at _www.bantamdell.com_ for ordering information.